Perilous Passage

Perilous Passage

B.J. BAYLE

A SANDCASTLE BOOK
A MEMBER OF THE DUNDURN GROUP
TORONTO

Editor: Michael Carroll
Design: Alison Carr
Printer: Webcom

Library and Archives Canada Cataloguing in Publication

Bayle, B. J. (Beverly J.)
Perilous passage / B.J. Bayle.

ISBN 978-1-55002-689-4

I. Title.

PS8553.A943P47 2007 jC813'.54 C2007-900864-X

1 2 3 4 5 11 10 09 08 07

Conseil des Arts du Canada Canada Council for the Arts

ONTARIO ARTS COUNCIL
CONSEIL DES ARTS DE L'ONTARIO

Canada

We acknowledge the support of **The Canada Council for the Arts** and the **Ontario Arts Council** for our publishing program. We also acknowledge the financial support of the **Government of Canada** through the **Book Publishing Industry Development Program** and **The Association for the Export of Canadian Books**, and the **Government of Ontario** through the **Ontario Book Publishers Tax Credit** program, and the **Ontario Media Development Corporation**.

Care has been taken to trace the ownership of copyright material used in this book. The author and the publisher welcome any information enabling them to rectify any references or credits in subsequent editions.

J. Kirk Howard, President

Printed and bound in Canada.
Printed on recycled paper.

www.dundurn.com

Dundurn Press
3 Church Street, Suite 500
Toronto, Ontario, Canada
M5E 1M2

Gazelle Book Services Limited
White Cross Mills
High Town, Lancaster, England
LA1 4XS

Dundurn Press
2250 Military Road
Tonawanda, NY
U.S.A. 14150

For the Bayle cheering section: Audrey, Nicole, Lauren, MaryBeth, Shawn, Chris, and two Hanks

ACKNOWLEDGEMENTS

My gratitude forever to my husband, Hank, who served as both chauffeur and cameraman when we attempted to follow the route taken by David Thompson and his brigades as they struggled to find the source of the Columbia River and a viable trade route to the Pacific Ocean. Our journey began at the impressive Rocky Mountain House National Historic Site with its wealth of information and ended at Astoria, Washington. I am grateful to the staff of the museums we visited along the way for their willingness to add to our information about Thompson — in particular those at the Windermere Valley Museum in Invermere, British Columbia; the Kettle Falls Historical Center at Kettle Falls, Washington; the Spokane House Interpretive Center in Spokane, Washington; and the Glenbow Museum in Calgary, Alberta.

I am also grateful to the Alberta Foundation for the Arts, which funded my research. Most of all, I owe many thanks to Michael Carroll, The Dundurn Group's editorial director, who with insight and hard work edits my stories and makes them better.

CHAPTER 1

He had become accustomed to the taunting from the innkeeper's two young sons. Now, ignoring their cries of "Peter No-Name," he plunged down the path leading to the small river that rushed to join the mighty St. Lawrence. Peter filled the two wooden buckets he carried and turned to climb back up to the bluff overlooking the growing settlement of Montreal. As he laboured upward, he noticed a stocky man with a dark beard standing at the top. The man had one booted foot propped on a large rock, elbow on his knee and chin in his hand, as he stared into the distance. His broad, muscular torso and heavy arms were almost out of proportion to his short legs, which told Peter the man was most likely one of the voyageurs who usually stayed at the inn at the end of a journey. The other clues were the fire-red shirt and the gaily striped yellow-and-red sash that he wore.

As Peter drew close, the voyageur flashed a friendly grin. The last section of the path was steeper, so Peter leaned one wooden bucket against the rock while he grasped the other with two hands. Swinging the heavy pail onto the boarded walkway, he turned to reach for the one by the rock and saw out of the corner of one eye the boys running toward him. Before he could react, Peter found himself tumbling backwards down the hill, drenched by the water flying out of the bucket bouncing behind him.

Pretending not to hear the laughter of the half-dozen men fishing from the river who had witnessed his fall, Peter jumped to his feet and reached for the fallen pail. He bent to the water, trying to ignore the pain where the pail had crashed into his ribs, and allowed the container to fill slowly. Stony-faced, he began to climb once more. Those who had laughed had returned to their own tasks, but above him the two youngsters were calling out, "No-Name, No-Name ain't got no brain."

Peter moved upward steadily, hoping the boys hadn't noticed that the second bucket was leaning against the rock near the top of the hill. He hoped in vain, though. Wearily, he saw his tormenters dart toward the bucket. They could keep this up for hours.

Still smiling, the voyageur stepped in front of the giggling boys. He addressed them in a patois — a mixture of English and French with words from Cree, Scots, and Irish thrown in, a language Peter was beginning to understand.

"Ho, mes amis," the man said. "I, too, am one to play games. I will join you." With those words the voyageur lifted the heavy bucket easily and with one hand tossed its contents onto the open-mouthed boys. Then he flung the bucket to the ground at their feet and, no longer smiling, suggested they go down to the river and fill it.

Aghast, Peter watched as the frightened boys stumbled down the hill, bucket in hand. They would tell the innkeeper and he would be blamed! With two hands clutching the second bucket, Peter stepped over the crest of the hill and placed it almost at the feet of the voyageur.

Before Peter could speak, the man asked, "You are Peter?" When Peter nodded, the voyageur hesitated for a moment before continuing. "I am Boulard. Tell me, *s'il vous plaît*, though you are no thicker than a small tree, you stand much higher than those who attack you. Higher still than me, Boulard. How is it that you do not teach these fellows better manners?"

As Peter tried to wring the water out of the too small, shabby brown shirt, he said, "They're kin to the innkeeper at Wharf's End. I dare not trouble them lest I lose my place there."

Boulard frowned and put a hand on Peter's shoulder. "Me, I have no wish to make difficulties for you." He thought for a moment. "Together we will approach this innkeeper and I will say, 'I, Boulard, am the bad man of this event.'"

Too late. Behind Boulard, Peter saw the rotund innkeeper trotting toward them, his scowling face red. "You, boy! The horses aren't watered, the chickens haven't been fed, and here you are gossiping!" Before Peter could reply, the irate man spied his sons struggling up the hill with the water bucket. The scarlet on his face quickly spread to his bald head. "And now I see my sons doing your work. That's too much. Collect your things and get out!"

"Monsieur," Boulard interjected, "I know you to be a man of reason. Perhaps you will allow me to explain what takes place here."

The innkeeper's face brightened immediately with an

oily smile. "Excuse me, Monsieur Boulard, for making you a witness to this lout's manner. He's done nothing to reward my charity and I've had enough of him."

"You will not reconsider?" Boulard asked.

The innkeeper folded his arms over his bulging stomach and set his jaw. "No, sir, I won't."

Boulard smiled. "Then, Monsieur Innkeeper, you are an imbecile." Taking Peter's arm, he marched him down the dirt road leading to the older part of the city.

Events happened fast when they reached the small house of Annette and Jacques Vallade, Boulard's friends. While Madame Vallade constantly refilled the tin plate in front of Peter with stew, he satisfied the curiosity of his new acquaintances between mouthfuls. "I don't recall much at all before I woke up on the ship that found me," he told them. "They told me the other seven in the longboat were dead."

After a brief silence, Boulard asked bluntly, "And you do not recall so much as your name?"

It was true he had no name except the one given to him by the captain of the ship that had found him half-dead in the drifting longboat. The captain and the sailors had been kind to him during the weeks it had taken to reach Montreal, each trying their best to help him regain his memory. But he couldn't remember anything — not even how he got the wide scar on the back of his head that stretched from one ear to the other.

"The crew took seawater and christened me Peter for a first name, but they couldn't agree on a last name." Peter smiled as he remembered. After several days of arguing, the crew had agreed that with his freckles, his speech, and hair that resembled summer wheat, Peter must be from England — Portsmouth perhaps or Yorkshire but certainly not London. It was the captain who had thought Peter was about fifteen when he was rescued. With a flourish the captain had written in the ship's log: "Peter, an Englishman, born in 1794."

With sympathy in his eyes Boulard reached over and touched Peter's shoulder. "It is said it was a ship of the North West Company that brought you here last year. It may take much time, but it is certain the company will learn the name of the vessel you were on before you were rescued. Then perhaps the mystery will be revealed."

Peter nodded. "That's why I haven't tried to find better work. I hoped travellers stopping at the inn might have word of a missing ship. It's been eight months now." He pushed away his plate and stood. "I thank you kindly for the food, but I best be going."

"Non, non!" the two Vallades chorused. "You will sleep here tonight, and in the morning we will see."

"Me, I have been thinking," Boulard said, tapping his forehead. He turned to Peter. "You care for the horses. Can you do more?"

At first Peter wasn't certain what was meant by the question. "I feed the chickens and pick up the eggs at the inn ..." Frowning a little, Boulard shook his head, then Peter suddenly understood. "I can read and write and do sums, and I like to draw things when I can get the paper, but I guess there's no need here for that."

Boulard threw up his hands. "Read and write and do sums! Now I am certain we will find a place for you."

"He is too long in his legs to be a voyageur," Vallade said, "and his arms resemble twigs."

With one meaty hand Boulard waved away Vallade's

words. "*Certainement*, but he would make a fine clerk."

"We were told only today there are more clerks in Montreal for the North West Company than they have use for," Vallade reminded his friend.

Boulard stroked his beard and pursed his lips. "I have more ambitious thoughts. Peter will travel with us to Rainy Lake. It is there I am to bring letters to Monsieur Thompson. If those at the post have no need for a clerk, our mapmaker will know what to do with our young friend."

Peter was having trouble following the conversation. "Who ... who's Monsieur Thompson?"

Boulard pretended astonishment. "Is it possible you have not heard of David Thompson, the famous explorer?"

Peter shook his head. "I don't think so."

"Then I must inform you." With Vallade interrupting now and then, Boulard explained that he had been in Fort Churchill twenty-six years ago when a small pale-faced boy named David Thompson was brought from England by a Hudson's Bay ship and deposited on the cold, rocky shore. Weeks later Boulard had watched as the lad stared after the departing ship until its sails were out of sight, then wiped his eyes and was never seen to cry again.

"He was, I think, even younger than you," Boulard said to Peter, "and I only two years more than that ..."

Peter's stomach was full, and the room was warm. Feeling his head begin to nod, he straightened his shoulders and blinked, hoping no one had noticed. Apparently, no one had, for Boulard's voice droned on.

Peter was only vaguely aware when Boulard's voice stopped. He opened his eyes briefly as he was helped to a pallet of robes in a corner by the fireplace, but he still heard Boulard speaking to Vallade. "We must begin early in the morning. The brigade leaves at midday, and for the trip our young friend must have pantaloons and a blouse without holes."

Vallade spoke more slowly. "Have you considered that Monsieur Thompson might feel disagreeable when he learns he must return to the mountains? He might be filled with anger and not wish to give attention to young Peter."

At that moment Peter slid into a sound sleep and didn't hear the reply.

The next morning passed in a blur. Permission for Peter to travel with the brigade had to be secured from the office of the North West Company, which was easily accomplished when Boulard casually mentioned David Thompson. However, it wasn't as easy to get the company clerk to let Peter purchase on credit. When the clerk finally agreed, Boulard helped Peter buy two pairs of heavy dark blue trousers, two coarse cotton shirts, and a pair of moccasin boots.

Peter's euphoria, which had come with the knowledge he would no longer be at the beck and call of the innkeeper or be teased by his sons, began to fade as he stood beside Boulard on the narrow wharf in front of the North West Company's two-storied wooden warehouse. Below, on the river, bobbed eight wide canoes. They were being loaded by men who looked much like Vallade and Boulard — short in the legs but broad in the chest and heavy in the arms. All had dark beards and hair partly hidden by what to Peter seemed to be stockings. As he watched the men, Peter began to doubt the wisdom of agreeing to a journey of several days. What if word arrived in Montreal of a ship lost at sea? Would anyone remember its name or from whence it came by the time he returned? And there was something about these boats. And the water. His stomach started to churn.

As though reading his thoughts, Boulard touched Peter's shoulder. "Me, I have left word with all houses that do business with ships. They promise to ask the questions you would ask yourself if you were in Montreal."

Peter smiled guiltily, reminding himself to be grateful that he had found a friend like Boulard. For the first time since the sailors who had rescued him had left Montreal, someone seemed to care about what happened to him. Straightening his shoulders, Peter pointed at the North West Company sign. "Last night you said you and Mr. Thompson were with the Hudson's Bay Company." He had heard talk of the fighting between the two companies.

Boulard grinned. "Do you not recall I told you the Hudson's Bay Company had agreed that Monsieur Thompson would no longer trade furs but instead find new rivers and mountains and make maps?"

Peter nodded.

"When they did not keep that promise, Monsieur Thompson packed his instruments, and we paid a visit to the North West Company. They were happy to see us, I can tell you."

"Time!" shouted the burly, hard-faced man who was directing the loading of the canoes.

Peter followed Boulard and Vallade to the edge of the water, his eyes sweeping over the river. The wind had come up, and small waves were rocking the heavily loaded craft in front of him. Closing his eyes, he imagined hanging on to a rail as a mountain of water poured over him. With that thought he grew cold and his legs buckled slightly.

As Vallade hopped into the canoe, the steersman laughed at Peter and asked, "Why do you wait? Does your lordship fear the river?"

The steersman would have said more, but the expression on Boulard's face silenced him. Putting a hand on Peter's back, Boulard gently eased him forward and whispered in his ear, "Me, I have never seen the ocean, *mon ami*, but I know it has much power, more than this river. If we encounter a storm, though, we make for shore pretty quick, I tell you."

The men waiting in the boats stared at Peter. He swallowed hard and reached for the hand Vallade held out to him.

CHAPTER 2

Even while paddling against the strong current, the voyageurs sang and made jokes. And when the wind blew in their favour, they hoisted sails and sat back to smoke their pipes. They hadn't travelled more than a few miles before Peter relaxed and began to enjoy himself. Sometimes the paddlers were silent and listened as intently as Peter when Boulard described the adventures he had shared with David Thompson when they journeyed over the prairies and woodlands, forever pushing north or west and building forts to trade for furs. Always Thompson made his maps of rivers, hills, and valleys.

A vision of a mist over a green hill dotted with white flowers appeared in Peter's head and vanished so quickly that he wondered if he had imagined it. He shook his head and listened to Vallade, who was speaking now. "I also have shared a dugout with this mapmaker. He is a good man and fair, though we must listen to him read from his Bible at the end of each day." Vallade glanced at Boulard. "I do not think Monsieur Thompson will be pleased to learn the company wants him to cross the mountains again instead of going to Montreal."

Boulard chuckled knowingly. "David will be pleased. All the while we were at Kootenay House he had to do what is expected of a partner of the company and build more houses to trade for furs. He never had time to search for the big river — the Columbia."

"Then how did he know it was there?" Peter asked.

"It has been spoken of many times by the men in the ships with big sails who passed the place where it smashes into the Pacific Ocean. Me, I have not seen that. Yet."

Vallade laughed. "You have caught the fever for searching for this river of mystery from Monsieur Thompson."

Boulard grew serious. "It is Madame Charlotte Thompson who will be unhappy about this news. And Fanny." He tapped his pipe on the side of the boat and put it into his vest pocket. "Fanny has only nine years. Our mapmaker wishes to place her in school in Montreal. David now has a farm nearby where they would live for one year to be certain she will be happy. I, Boulard, agreed to travel ahead to arrange for this school, and this I did often by dogsled, for much of the rivers were covered with ice." He shrugged. "But I think now David's family will not see Montreal this year."

Except for the clouds of black flies that often hovered over their boats, Peter found the trip exciting. They travelled north up the Ottawa River to the Mattawa River, down that river to Lake Nipissing, then a little south along the French River and into Lake Huron's Georgian Bay and from there into the vastness of a beautiful lake called Superior. Most of the time the paddlers sang as they dipped their oars in the water. Peter marvelled at the voyageurs' strength every time it was necessary to unload the boats and carry them and each ninety-pound pack of goods overland during one of the many portages. They never seemed to complain. Peter didn't complain, either — not aloud. But when weeks passed with no sign of a fort or anything except a few Indian camps, he began to wonder if the post at Rainy Lake — their destination — really existed.

As they rinsed their cups and plates one cold morning, Vallade spoke his thoughts. "It is my hope that Monsieur Thompson will greet us at Grand Portage tomorrow night."

Boulard playfully punched his companion in the chest. "It is too early for the festivities, *mon ami*. I am not certain he will wait for them to arrive."

Vallade appeared disappointed. "It is now June and the ice has left the rivers. It is certain the brigades carrying the provisions are following us, and those from the north will be swiftly descending to Grand Portage with the current. Thus we will meet and celebrate."

Boulard shook his head. "I have lost track of the days, but you forget that our small canoes that are carrying only mail for Grand Portage and goods for the Rainy Lake post are much faster than the big ones. We will arrive too soon for the celebrations."

Vallade sighed and looked at Peter. "There is great feasting and dancing in the nights when the brigades from the north and west meet those from the east."

Peter glanced at Boulard, who explained. "The brigades — as many as thirty perhaps — from the north and the west carry the furs our Indian friends bring to them in winter, and those from the east bring supplies and trade goods for the next winter. These arrive in

Montreal on the great ships, and the great ships take back the furs across the ocean to England."

Peter nodded, thinking that this arrangement was very sensible. He had seen heavily laden canoes arrive in Montreal and wondered from whence they came.

Shortly before the voyageurs reached their destination, they swung their eight canoes into shore. Then, with much joking and laughing, the paddlers put on red-tasseled caps and bright sashes, but Vallade didn't get his wish. There were only a few canoes at Grand Portage when they arrived, though there was a small celebration nevertheless. Peter and his new friends were treated to a bountiful meal of potatoes, beef, and fish. He found it a welcome change from their daily fare of pork, pemmican, and maize. There was no word of David Thompson, and in the morning they were off again.

Although the post at Rainy Lake wasn't large, the small wharf was crowded with dozens of wide birchbark canoes. "It is the flotilla from the west," Boulard said, a broad smile lighting his eyes. "Monsieur Thompson will be with that one."

Peter's stomach flip-flopped. After leaving Grand Portage, Boulard had revealed his plan. "Observe, Peter. I, Boulard, have been thinking. When we encounter Monsieur Thompson, I will request you lodge with us in Rocky Mountain House for the winter where you will learn to be a company man. In the spring when we go back to the mountains to find this mysterious river, maybe you will accompany us. Though perhaps you will choose to be a clerk at the post. I, myself, will present you to David."

Even though Peter had still found himself more

than a little bewildered by the change in his life since he had met Boulard, he had nodded agreement. After all, he trusted his new friend. Besides, what choice did he have?

Now, determined to make a good impression, his heart thumping, he climbed from the rocking craft and fell face forward onto the muddy shore. He scrambled to his feet, afraid to look up for fear everyone on the landing had witnessed his clumsiness. Apparently, no one had except for the family being greeted by Boulard.

A squarely built, solemn-faced man glanced down at Peter once, then ripped open one of the letters Boulard had handed to him. Peter groaned. This must be David Thompson, with his wife and two of his children! He tried to brush off the mud clinging to his breeches, but only succeeded in rubbing it into the cloth. Worrying that he might have mud on his face, as well, he stood back and waited to be presented, but Boulard appeared to have forgotten him. He watched the explorer scan the document in his hand.

Finally, the man's face broke into a smile, and he clapped Boulard on the shoulder. "At last, old friend, those blockheads in Parliament have realized it is time to claim the land beyond the mountains before the Americans take it for themselves. We'll return to the Columbia district immediately — this time to find the great river to the west and, I pray, a good safe passage to the Pacific Ocean."

He turned to his wife. "Think of it, Charlotte. You recall while at Kootenay House we learned that farther west the furs are richer and more plentiful. Our company could double in size and profit if we establish trading places along that great passage. Our ships from London could round this continent and take the furs on to China. Men who sailed with Captain Cook reported furs fetching astonishing prices in the Far East."

"This great river," the small woman said softly, "is the one you spoke of that Alexander Mackenzie and Simon Fraser couldn't find?"

"True," Thompson said, smiling at his wife. "But they didn't have the good sextant and compass I now have. Nor, and I'm not boasting, are they my equals as surveyors. I'm convinced they were too far north, and though they did find rivers to the sea, they were impossible for use with loaded canoes."

"And if you find this great river, then you will finish your map." It was a statement, not a question, and her voice was full of hope.

As they talked, Peter studied the family. The boy clinging to his mother Peter surmised to be Samuel. Standing erectly was a girl who was the image of her mother. He decided this must be Fanny, who was to go to school in Montreal. She looked younger than nine. Like her mother, she was quite small. Above her softly rounded cheekbones her eyes, too, were set wide apart and were the colour of russet autumn leaves, while the skin on her arms was lighter than her mother's. Peter recalled Vallade saying that Madame Thompson had a Cree mother, but that her father was a Scottish partner in the North West Company who had sailed back to England, leaving his family behind. That would make Charlotte Thompson half-Scottish and half-Cree, and her daughter a combination of both mixed with the Welsh ancestry of David Thompson.

Peter smiled when it crossed his mind that Fanny was fortunate to look more like her mother than her father whose cleanly shaven jaw was square and heavy, making him appear quite stern. Below the explorer's dark hair, which hung to his bushy eyebrows, were piercing blue eyes.

When Charlotte murmured Fanny's name in a question, he couldn't hear everything she said, but he saw the light go out of Thompson's eyes. The explorer hesitated a moment, then gestured toward a family stepping into one of the canoes pointed to the east. A tall man dressed in buckskins got in first, then helped in an Indian woman with two children who clutched her bright red cotton skirt. They were followed by a tall boy.

"Mr. McCalfie," Thompson said, "and his family travel east with the brigade. They'll put their son in school as we mean to do with Fanny. I know him to be a good man — honest and responsible. I'll ask that he look after Fanny until they reach Montreal. There our friend Alex Fraser and his good wife will see to her needs."

Charlotte nodded, then straightened her shoulders as she turned to Fanny. Peter felt a lump in his throat as mother and daughter talked quietly hand in hand while the afternoon sunlight painted their skin golden. He slipped carefully back to the canoe and reached inside for the bag holding his goods. Inside was a roll of precious paper and his charcoal sticks. He returned to the dock and, careful to keep himself screened by the clerks and voyageurs counting and packing bales into the boats, he started to sketch.

Boulard and the explorer returned from their discussion with McCalfie, and the last bit of cargo was carefully placed in a canoe. The paddlers lifted their oars and began to sing. Peter was oddly comforted when he saw Fanny being held closely in the arms of plump Mrs. McCalfie. When the last canoe disappeared from sight, Boulard motioned for Peter to wait when he followed Thompson into the log building.

An elderly Cree woman stood near Charlotte holding an infant and shushing a toddler while Fanny's mother stared at the river. These two children, Boulard had told Peter, were John and Emma, Thompson's other offspring. Taking a deep breath, Peter approached the group. "Excuse me, ma'am. I'd be obliged if you'd accept this." He held out the sketch he had made of Fanny.

Charlotte looked at him blankly, then peered at the drawing. With a gasp she snatched the paper and studied the face of her daughter. Glancing up at Peter, then back at the picture, she sobbed once and stepped forward to hug him.

Not knowing what to do, Peter put his arms around her awkwardly and let her cry. Over her shoulder he saw Thompson striding toward them, his face darkened by a scowl.

Peter released his hold on the explorer's wife, but before he could explain his arm was grasped roughly and Thompson growled, "What is this? What ..."

Smiling through her tears, Charlotte said, "David, look. Look at the gift this young man gave me." As she spoke, she thrust the drawing in front of her husband's eyes. "It's a picture."

"Picture?" Thompson barked. "A picture of what?"

"Of our Fan. Look."

Releasing Peter, Thompson took the paper and

stared at it for a long moment before he handed it to Boulard. "You have proved me wrong, my friend. This young man may be useful, after all. It would save me much time if he could draw the plants and animals in my journals, thus freeing me of the task of describing them in detail." He didn't smile, but his eyes twinkled when he added, "Perhaps it's just as well that my wife will stay east of the mountains."

"David, no!" Charlotte protested.

Her husband nodded. "It must be so. There will be little time to rest on this journey over the mountains. Also, you're with child again. It will be better for you, Samuel, Emma, John, and the new baby to rest with your brother and mother at Whitemud House."

When Thompson led his family into the trade room, Peter turned to Boulard and tried to thank him for his help. The voyageur's eyes were troubled. "There is much I did not know, Peter. I thought to have you aid Monsieur Thompson in his making of maps in a warm cabin in the long days of winter, which will arrive soon enough. Today I learn he does not wish to wait for next spring to cross the mountains."

Peter was silent and confused. Finally, he asked, "What does that mean, Boulard? Am I to return to Montreal now?"

Boulard shrugged. "If that is your wish. There will be other brigades with cargo to bring to the east in which I can arrange for you to travel. I have no fear the chief trader here will find work for you to do while you wait."

Peter's heartbeat quickened as he pondered his dilemma. He would be alone again — no friends, no family. If he continued with Boulard and Thompson, he wouldn't be alone, but he would be far from Montreal when the name of the ship that had sunk and from whence it had come was discovered. Still, he shook his head and whispered, "I don't want to go back."

Boulard grinned hugely and clapped Peter on the shoulder. Taking a large red kerchief from his pocket, he dusted a corner of the wharf before seating himself, then motioned for Peter to sit beside him. "Before you are certain of your decision, you must be told of the dangers and hardships of the journey."

Peter nodded slowly. "Vallade said the Peigans are Indians who live far to the west in the foothills of the great mountains and that they're fierce warriors and collectors of horses."

"That is true. It is my opinion that they often try to collect the horse even while one is seated on it."

"Then there's danger from the Peigans?"

Boulard shook his head. "Not so much all Peigans, though we are careful not to offend them. With Monsieur Thompson I once wintered with them. We are friends with the paramount chief, who is much respected by his people. It is not so with the war chief, who is now unhappy with us. He learns we take guns over the mountains, so their rivals the Kootenays can hunt and defend themselves."

Hesitantly, Peter asked, "Will we see this war chief?"

Boulard shrugged. "Perhaps. We load up at Rocky Mountain House as always. We paddle fifty miles upriver to Howse Pass through the mountains where the North Saskatchewan River begins. Many Peigans trade with us at Rocky Mountain House, and they camp not far from this river. They know when traders go to the mountains, but until now they have not tried to stop us before we reach the pass. This has been true for three years. Praise God it will always be so."

Peter's throat was dry, and his voice squeaked as he said, "You told me I must be able to fire a musket, but I don't think I ever have."

"Yes, you must learn much. It will not be as I thought. You will not have many months to learn our ways. I do not agree with my friend David when he chooses to begin our journey as soon as we are prepared. It is possible we will cross the big mountains when they are covered with snow and ice." He peered into Peter's eyes. "You have not felt cold such as we will experience, nor venture on trails so formidable. I will see that you are dressed as we ourselves will be, but still you will find your hands and feet so cold they will be without feeling."

Peter closed his eyes as a flash of memory shot into his head and he felt himself running down an icy path while his feet burned with the cold. The image disappeared quickly, but he kept his eyes shut, hoping more would appear. However, there was nothing. Biting his lip, he opened his eyes and darted a glance at Boulard.

"Do you recall something, *mon ami*?" the voyageur asked.

Peter stood and squared his shoulders. "No, but I'm not giving up on remembering how I got here. It won't matter where I am when that happens. I feel grateful that you and Mr. Thompson are willing to take me with you."

"Bien," Boulard said, rising to his feet. "Now we will inform Monsieur Thompson and prepare for the long trip up these waters."

CHAPTER 3

Boulard wasn't joking about the long journey. It took weeks to reach Whitemud House. Most of the trip was without incident except for a violent storm as they passed along the shores of Lake Winnipeg. True to his word, Boulard pointed the nose of their canoe to the shore, and the rest of the boat brigade followed. They camped until noon the next day when the fury of the wind and rain lessened. A week later they were painfully peppered with hail when they portaged at the Narrows.

Although the days passed slowly, they were broken almost daily by encounters with huge fur-laden canoes travelling downstream to Grand Portage. At these times the vessels would turn toward shore and news would be exchanged by the voyageurs without leaving their boats. Thompson kept these intervals short, for it was plain to see he was impatient to reach Whitemud House.

Boulard was never too busy steering their craft around the rocks in the river to answer Peter's questions about the ever-changing landscape and the wild creatures they saw. Huge flocks of geese rose in clouds when they were disturbed by the songs of the paddlers, and ducks flapped overhead as did high-flying cranes, identified only by their throaty cries. It was the long-legged antlered creatures that interested Peter most, for he was certain he had never seen them before. Once a half-dozen dog-like creatures darted from their drinking spot when the canoes appeared. Boulard called them prairie wolves.

About the time Peter began to yearn for the wretched straw bed he had slept on in the Montreal inn's stable rather than continue to suffer the stony shoreline of the North Saskatchewan, Boulard announced they would spend that night in Whitemud House. *House* wasn't exactly the term Peter would have chosen for the string of low-roofed log buildings with holes for windows. They were half surrounded by brightly decorated tents that Boulard called tipis. Small brown-faced children were shouting, followed by equally noisy dogs as they rushed to greet the canoes.

"Here is your home, but not for many days, Peter," Boulard said with a grin.

Peter stared unseeingly at his friend as the enormity of what he had undertaken swept over him, and for a moment he wanted to be anywhere except here in this strange land. Realizing Boulard was looking at him questioningly, Peter managed a faint grin, then bent to gather his packet of paper and spare clothing. As he stepped into the shallow water along the shore of the North Saskatchewan, he fixed a smile on his face and prepared to greet the knot of adults and children rushing toward them. They ignored Boulard and him, however, in favour of the canoe containing David Thompson and his family.

The explorer wasted little time on greetings and instead beckoned to Boulard and Peter to follow him into the largest of the line of rooms that were almost filled with boxes and barrels. Peter learned later that these contained trade goods that would be purchased on credit by the Blackfoot for the coming winter.

Thompson had scarcely spoken to Peter during the lengthy expedition up the North Saskatchewan, but now he turned to him. "Boulard will see that you have all you need for the journey. These goods will be your pay for now, but if you prove your worth, you'll receive more pay at the end." Ignoring Peter's stammered thanks, the explorer turned to Boulard. "We leave when our provisions arrive. While we wait, see that Peter is able to sit a horse and to handle a musket."

Peter discovered he had no trouble mastering the tall chestnut mare he was given, even though she snorted and danced around, resenting an interruption in her feeding. The gun was a different matter, though. It took several attempts to load the thing, and a dozen more to hit Boulard's big bandana only twenty feet away. When that was finally accomplished, Peter learned to pack a horse and put up a tent.

Once he was invited to the Thompson family's roomy cabin to aid Charlotte in the preparation of an alphabet book so she could teach six-year-old Samuel to read. On the table was a copy of Oliver Goldsmith's novel *The Vicar of Wakefield*, with a bookmark protruding from it. When he saw the book, a veil appeared in his mind's eye, and through it he saw a lamp burning on a rough table, its glow illuminating a book beside it.

"I've read this book!" Peter cried. "I know I have."

Although the vision had lasted only an instant, he was delighted. Eagerly, Charlotte began to discuss the novel's plot, and Peter had to force himself to respond. He was much more interested in trying to imagine the lamp and the table again and perhaps the room where they stood. Charlotte's enthusiasm for the book had diminished her natural shyness. Sensing this, Peter reluctantly let go of his vision and concentrated on her words.

"The company doesn't wish women to be taught to read, but my husband taught me, anyway," she said proudly. "Also Fanny and I will teach the rest of the children. David wants us to be prepared for living in Montreal." She sighed, and her voice dropped as she added, "After he finds his great river, that is."

Peter took his leave then and later found Boulard beside an overturned canoe that he was caulking with heated pine tar. Accustomed now to helping with tasks without being told, Peter found a flat stick and dipped it into the sticky black substance. "Boulard, if David Thompson is a partner in the North West Company, why does he have to be the one to find this Columbia River? Why couldn't he send someone else and go to Montreal with his little girl?"

Boulard stopped applying the tar on the seams of the canoe and turned to Peter, his eyebrows raised almost to the black hair that hung on his forehead. "Send another? Peter, after all I have told you of David Thompson, you still do not understand that finding in the big mountains the beginning of this magic river and thus a route to the ocean is of the greatest importance to him. He wishes to do so for the company he serves, but more than that, he will be able to finish his map of this land. For David maps have been his life from his very first days in this country."

When Peter wandered into the trade room, there was no doubt in his mind that Thompson was a full partner in the company when he heard him speaking to Alexander Henry, the chief trader of Whitemud House. "Charlotte is to charge whatever provisions she needs to my account, and see to it that she and her mother are well supplied with wood and water."

Peter was startled to hear Henry's reply. "You spoil your woman, man, and the rest of the women know it. This very morning my own wife demanded I cook the morning meal and clean the pots."

Thompson smiled slightly. "And I suppose you burned the pots when you scorched her kippers and eggs."

Both men burst into laughter, and Henry said, "Kippers and eggs! I've been in this wilderness so long that I've forgotten what they taste like."

Peter frowned. Thompson's laughter was an unfamiliar sound. He had heard some of the paddlers grumble that the mapmaker was a dry stick of a man — and too strict with his rules. And it was said the other partners in the company were annoyed that he didn't drink spirits and refused to take alcohol across the mountains for trade with the Indians there. Lost in thought, Peter jumped when Thompson turned and called out, "There you are, Peter. I wish to speak with you. I'm pleased to hear that you're handling your horse well, since you'll ride with me and two of our hunters while the rest of the company takes to the canoes."

As Peter wondered if he was expected to thank the man or be truthful and say he would prefer to go in the canoe with Boulard, Thompson solved his quandary by turning to Henry and continuing their conversation. "When last I came from across the mountains, the Peigans showed me no unfriendliness. Why do you think we might have trouble this time as we go up the river?"

Henry shrugged. "You said yourself that Finan McDonald wasn't the man to care for business at Kootenay House, and from what I hear, you were right. He went hunting with some of the Flatheads and, not knowing their enemies now have guns, the Peigans tried to ambush them. Five of their own were killed in the battle, and they blame McDonald for two of those. It's certain the Peigans will take exception to our people arming the Kootenays or any other of their adversaries."

"You might," Thompson said, "have no trouble from the Peigans when you reopen Rocky Mountain House if you make it clear you're there to trade with them only. They have need of the goods you'll be bringing."

With a heavy heart Peter left the trade room to think about what he had just heard. Travelling on snow and ice and crossing mountains were enough to make anyone figure they ought not to be here, but shooting at people and having them shoot back ... He shook his head and shivered.

CHAPTER 4

It was early September by the time the brigade of four wide-bottomed canoes pushed off carrying trade goods and more than twenty men — three of them with their Cree wives. Peter turned his horse to follow Thompson and the two Iroquois hunters the explorer had hired — Red Blanket and Young Joseph. Sitting tall astride his dancing mount, Peter was terrified he might sniffle. It hadn't been easy to wave goodbye to Boulard, who had said in parting, "Perhaps as you ride through the forests you will find that which you do not recall."

Hearing those words had made Peter's heart beat a little faster, even though his head had reminded him that most likely such a thing wouldn't happen.

The riders followed a trail away from the North Saskatchewan into the deep woods. Thompson had instructed Boulard to meet them three days hence, at which time the brigade would be supplied with the meat his hunters had shot. The riders spread out. Red Blanket and Young Joseph took separate trails, while Peter remained with the explorer and led the two packhorses. Peter had been told that Thompson usually preferred to hunt by himself, but he realized now that their leader spent more time on his journals than he did hunting. A dozen times before the day was over he paused to instruct Peter to quickly sketch a berry-laden bush or the dying leaves on a thicket of trees. Neither he nor Thompson spotted so much as a rabbit, nor did the other men.

When the four hunters camped on the second night, Thompson expressed concern to the Iroquois. "This forest had red deer aplenty only a year past. Why are they scarce now?"

"Peigans good hunters," Red Blanket said. "They are many."

Peter spoke to Young Joseph in a hushed tone. "If they see us, will they be friendly?"

"They won't trouble us if they find us hunting," Thompson said from across the fire, "because they'll see we carry no guns to trade with their enemies."

"Tomorrow we will find game," Young Joseph said confidently.

Thompson rose and reached for his bedroll. "Men who are hungry can't paddle far upstream. We must find meat tomorrow."

That night Peter felt pangs of hunger himself. Certain they would kill their meat along the way, they hadn't packed enough for three days, and he had to be content with a small slice of the salt pork sent from England, which he detested, and two potatoes. Thompson took even less, giving his share of the meat to the two Indians. Without knowing how or when he had learned to set snares, Peter did so before crawling into his bedroll. In the morning they dined on three rabbits caught in the traps.

Red Blanket only grunted his approval, but Thompson

said, "Well done, Peter."

Although he tried to appear nonchalant, Peter couldn't help grinning after the unaccustomed praise.

Later in the day Young Joseph and Red Blanket followed the sounds of a battle between two heavily antlered red deer and shot both unsuspecting animals. Thompson shot a doe cleanly behind the ear and could have killed a medium-sized black bear that was upwind munching on red berries. Instead he gestured to Peter to dismount and secure his horse. Then they crept closer to the bear and hid themselves behind a stout spruce tree.

"I'd like to have a drawing of this one," Thompson whispered, "but be as quiet as you can."

Swiftly, Peter made a rough sketch while Thompson explained. "A creature such as this would supply us with much meat, but the bear is an important part of the religion of the Iroquois and I don't want to offend our companions."

Peter listened with satisfaction. Helping Thompson clean the deer he had shot had been bad enough. He tried not to think of what gutting a bear would be like.

The two Iroquois had a crackling fire going at their camp beside the river when Peter and Thompson arrived at almost the same moment as the brigade did.

"Ho!" Boulard shouted from the bow of the first canoe. "I see you have done well. We have meat still for a feast tonight, and it appears you have enough for three, maybe four days more."

"Bien!" Vallade cried as he followed Boulard from the canoe. "Enough for a fete when next we meet at Rocky Mountain House."

The mapmaker shook his head. "The House has been

closed for some time. Mr. Henry hasn't arrived yet to open it again for trade. We'll swing wide into the forest tomorrow to avoid the deep gullies along the river, and we won't see you again until we meet where Porcupine Creek empties into our river."

If Vallade was disappointed, he didn't show it, but Peter couldn't help thinking it would have been good to sleep under a roof for one night. The sudden, short bursts of light rain that had soaked their tents on two of the nights they had camped were icy cold.

The women went into the forest to gather more wood while the men unloaded the packhorses. After trying to help and discovering he wasn't needed, Peter perched on a flat rock and prepared to add to his sketches. With the setting sun at his back and the smell of roasting meat wafting from the fire, he heaved a sigh of contentment. For the first time in almost a year, finding his name and his past wasn't foremost in his mind.

For the next three days they rode, scarcely searching for game. They wanted to be closer to their meeting with the brigade before making a kill so the meat would be fresh. On the third day Young Joseph shot a red deer and Thompson got a mule deer. While they stopped to dress the carcasses, Red Blanket continued to hunt and met them with another red deer and four rabbits. It took the rest of the day to transport the meat through the woods to a hill above the confluence of the Porcupine River and the North Saskatchewan. That night they ate well, and once more Peter went to sleep with a feeling of wellbeing. *This is a good journey,* he told himself, *better even than in the canoe, for then I was almost a child and now I'm one of the men.*

Some of Peter's good cheer evaporated the next night when they rolled into their blankets, knowing the brigade should have arrived by now and wondering why it hadn't. When he awoke in the morning, he had a sense of uneasiness strong enough for him to want little of the roasted rabbit, though he drank some of Thompson's precious tea.

Red Blanket, too, ate little and stared into the distance without speaking. When the Iroquois finished, he rose and pointed at the meat hanging in the trees. "I have dreamed of what will happen. No man of the brigade will eat that meat." Without another word he strode to his horse and rode away.

Thompson inhaled, sighed deeply, and turned to Young Joseph. "I didn't dream anything. Even so, Peter and I will ride back along the river to learn what delays our canoes. If I find them, I will fire my musket as a signal for you to reload the packhorses and start down to the river."

As they mounted their horses, Peter asked, "Is it possible the brigade went on ahead upstream?"

To Peter's relief Thompson replied without a trace of impatience. "It may be possible they missed the meeting place, but I don't think so. Boulard knows it well."

To avoid the deep gullies that led to the river and still not miss the canoes, they left the shelter of the trees, and Thompson led the way down to the shallow water along the edge of the river. The sky was darkening, and the tang of snow was in the air when he halted suddenly and dismounted, motioning for Peter to do the same. Pointing at the horizon, he said, "Peigan tents."

The tops of more than a dozen tipis protruded

above the low hill far ahead. Gesturing for Peter to follow, Thompson led his horse back upstream. When he signalled it was safe, they mounted again and rode upward into the trees hugging the river. After they tied their horses to sturdy trees, Thompson jerked his musket from its battered scabbard and told Peter to do the same. His expression grim, the mapmaker said, "We'll need these if we find they have our brigade captive."

Peter's mouth had become too dry to form words, but he managed to nod. With weapons loaded they slipped through the trees, climbing in and out of the deep gullies as they moved closer to the Peigan camp. Peter's heart hammered as he stumbled behind Thompson, and it nearly leaped out of his chest when the mapmaker stopped abruptly and pointed to a pile of rocks at the edge of the river. One was spattered with blood.

CHAPTER 5

Quickly, Peter and Thompson scrambled up one of the tall cliffs that jutted out of the forest above the river, then lay on their stomachs to study the Indian camp in the distance. "I see no sign of our people," Thompson said. "And the Peigans don't appear to have scouts on guard. They would if they had reason to fear the company would be looking for its people."

The explorer turned and inched down the steep hill, with Peter following cautiously until they plunged into the tangled forest at the bottom. Hoping Thompson wasn't as lost as he was, Peter ignored the scratches from the thorns on the tall brush and hurried to keep his companion in sight until he saw the dark shadows of the two horses.

Bridle in one hand and weapon in the other, Peter vaulted into his saddle. At that same moment the nervous animal swung sideways, causing Peter to topple to the ground on one side and his gun on the other. As the musket landed, it fired, the roar reverberating through the trees.

The wind knocked out of him, Peter lay still for a moment, but with Thompson's "Thunderation!" he jumped to his feet, terrified he might have wounded the explorer or his horse. Relief clashed with dread when he saw Thompson glaring beside him and holding the reins of both horses. Without a word Peter dropped to his knees to search for his musket in the darkening woods.

Thompson spoke then, his words sounding as though he were grinding them through his teeth. "Leave it! Get on your horse! The Peigans will want to know who fired that shot, and added to that, Young Joseph might think it was a signal to bring down the meat."

It was completely dark when they reached their camp and reported to Young Joseph, who listened impassively. "The Peigans cannot track in the dark. They will wait for daybreak."

Heartsick at not being more careful, Peter barely slept. He could hear Thompson tossing restlessly on his pallet nearby.

The next morning in the murky light between darkness and dawn they led the stumbling horses over fallen logs and pushed their way through tall brush that tore at their clothing. To Peter it seemed they were moving uphill with agonizing slowness and in a wide circle, always looking back over their shoulders into the shadowy forest behind them.

There was no break of day. The dense, dark clouds hid the sun. Peter's arms ached with the effort of tugging the reins of his horse as he urged it around boulders and over fallen trees. It felt as if they had been leading the animals for hours when they came upon a wide stream rushing downward. They were able to mount then and allow the animals to pick their way in the shallow edge of the water.

Hopefully, Peter spoke over his shoulder to Young Joseph. "Even the Peigans shouldn't be able to track us now."

The Iroquois didn't answer.

Hours later, when the first fat snowflakes began to fall, Thompson decided with obvious reluctance that it was time to rest the weary horses. Peter guided his mount to a patch of tall grass and slid to the ground to hobble to the river. The toes on his left foot throbbed with pain, the result of trudging through the woods in the unaccustomed stiff leather boots. As he pulled off the offending boot to wriggle his toes in the icy stream, the silence was shattered by the roar of a musket.

In spite of his own shock of surprise, Peter was aware of the reactions of his companions. Behind him Thompson had leaped ahead to snatch the reins of his horse as well as the two packhorses, but Young Joseph had disappeared. Peter saw that his own mount was moving nervously through the trees, trailing the reins. Grabbing his boot and ignoring the pain in his foot, he limped through the trees after her. It was then that he heard a second gunshot, though much farther away.

It was snowing more heavily now, and not wanting to become separated from his companions, Peter tugged at his horse and moved toward the sounds of the river. He had taken two steps when Thompson appeared at his side. "Stay here," the explorer whispered. "Young Joseph left us to find who fired the musket. Perhaps it was a man of the brigade."

"Maybe it was the Peigans following us," Peter volunteered, trying to prevent his voice from shaking.

Thompson moved away without replying.

It seemed longer, but it was less than two hours before Young Joseph returned, his usually sober face wearing a grim smile. "They do not find our trail. The gunfire was to signal to find their way back to the river."

Peter and his companions rode slowly, following this new river downstream until it was dark again. When they camped, they allowed themselves a small fire. Young Joseph rolled up in his blanket only minutes after he swallowed the last strip of deer meat and fell asleep. Peter was relieved. He knew he was due for a stern tongue lashing for causing their trouble, and he preferred Young Joseph wasn't witness to it. He moved to sit on a log and wrapped himself in a blanket just as the explorer came back into the firelight carrying a small kettle.

Thompson squatted by the fire. "I have water to make tea, Peter. It will warm us more than our blankets."

Peter darted a quick look at the explorer. Thompson was speaking to him, and not in anger. His thoughts were hopeful. "Sir ..." he began stiffly. "I know I ... I'm sorry for the —"

With a wave of his hand Thompson dismissed the apology. "You only had an accident, whereas I've been foolishly careless."

Peter was astonished. He hadn't thought of Thompson as someone who ever owned up to making a mistake. Or of being careless.

The explorer poked at the fire with a long stick to make a level place for the kettle. "Thinking it would be safer, I wrapped my compass and placed it in the iron box in the canoe." He gestured toward the river. "I believe this may be the Brazeau — it's of sufficient size — but it may not be. If I'm right, it will meet with the North

Saskatchewan some two days' ride downstream from Rocky Mountain House. From the House we'll follow it upstream until we find our brigade." He paused to sip his tea and stare into the fire. "We must find our men."

Peter's heart dropped below his belt. David Thompson — the great mapmaker — wasn't certain where they were now! He took a deep, shaky breath, but when his companion turned to look at him Peter tried to speak confidently. "If the sun is up tomorrow, it should be a lot easier to know which way to go."

Thompson made no comment, and they drank their tea in silence.

A grey dawn revealed that they had been covered with a blanket of snow while they had slept, but the clouds were thinning and weak rays of the sun were finding their way through the trees. Peter stuck his head out of his blankets and saw Young Joseph pulling thin strips of wood from a pack to make a fire while he listened to Thompson.

"You're certain you'll have no trouble finding the Kootenay Plain?" Thompson asked.

Young Joseph grunted an inaudible reply and knelt to strike flint against stone. Thompson waited while the Iroquois blew gently on the tiny flame. When he appeared satisfied that his fire had started, he stood. "I know these woods. I will leave my horse here."

Thompson nodded. "Tell Bercier to bring all the horses to where the Brazeau meets the great river and wait there. Tell him to watch for the Peigans."

Peter shrugged off his blankets and looked around, then sat upright. Rubbing his eyes, he asked, "Where's Young Joseph going? Who's Bercier?"

"Bercier cares for the horses we'll need when we reach the mountains. He drove them to the Kootenay Plain long before we began our journey and expects to wait there for the brigade." Thompson paused, looking thoughtful. Finally, he said, "I fear the Peigans will no longer allow us to journey freely up the North Saskatchewan. We must find another way through the mountains."

"But Boulard told me the Peigans are your friends."

"Some are, but I fear the brigade was attacked by those who aren't. It vexes me to believe they may have drawn the blood of one of our men. Armed as we are, we might easily defeat them, but fighting would only mean children without fathers for them and more trouble for us."

After a hurried meal of a few strips of deer meat and the dried berries Charlotte had packed, Young Joseph tied his blanket in a roll, slung it over his shoulder, and picked up his musket. Thompson attached a pouch containing more meat to the blanket roll and handed the Iroquois a small bag. "You may need this extra powder and shot, my friend, though I pray you won't."

Young Joseph nodded and placed a hand on the explorer's shoulder. He stood there for a moment, then turned and disappeared into the trees.

Peter looked after him anxiously. "How does he know which trail to take?"

Thompson stirred the campfire. "Many years past, Young Joseph's forefathers came from the east with fur traders and settled in the forests at the foot of the mountains. They know these rivers and hills very well."

When Thompson stood, Peter gestured to the rushing water. "The river's getting a bit wider. Does Young Joseph believe this is the Brazeau?"

"The Iroquois have different names for the mountains and rivers than we do, but this morning he said this was the only large river in these parts. I feel it must be the one we seek." Thompson turned to the tethered horses. "We're long past the time to bring meat to the brigade, and if they fear to hunt for themselves lest they attract hostile Peigans, the men will be hungry indeed. This red deer we have would be most welcome."

During the next few days, as the stream they followed widened into a fast-moving river fed by the dozens of small creeks and rivulets they forded, Peter saw Thompson grow more confident about their whereabouts. He lost track of the number of days they rode through the trees along the river while leading the unruly packhorses. Then, finally, they discovered a break in the forest at the top of a hill. Far in the distance, light from the setting sun glinted off a tiny ribbon of water. Before Peter could ask the question, Thompson was peering through his telescope. "It's my belief we've found the North Saskatchewan, lad."

Peter was too choked with relief to reply.

Thompson closed his telescope. "It's too far away for us to try to reach it tonight. At first light we'll start. With luck, by nightfall tomorrow, we'll camp beside it."

While speaking, Thompson slid from his horse and led it and the packhorses to the water to drink, then moved upstream to fill his teakettle. Kneeling on a large rock, he turned to Peter to speak when the rock suddenly rolled and the explorer cried out. Not knowing his companion was in trouble, Peter scrambled after the kettle floating downstream and returned to find the mapmaker bent awkwardly, one knee jammed between two boulders and his face contorted with pain.

Without hesitating Peter jumped into water that reached to his knees and clawed at the smaller stones around one of the large rocks. Then he used all his strength to push it away from the trapped knee. With shaking hands he stripped his bedroll from a packhorse and yanked a blanket from it to stretch on the ground before he helped Thompson onto the damp earth. Taking a second blanket, he covered him and then searched for flint and rock to start a fire. All the while, Thompson was silent, eyes closed, face white. With trembling hands Peter managed to strike sparks over the slivers of wood and bark that he had been told to carry, and quickly had a fire to warm his companion.

Thompson opened his eyes. With one arm propping himself, he rose to a half-sitting position. "In the pack behind my saddle you'll find a small box. Bring that and a cup of water."

Peter quickly found the box and followed Thompson's instructions. He unrolled an oilskin pouch and handed it to the explorer, then watched as Thompson shook a small amount into his mouth of what appeared to be finely chopped tree bark. Handing back the pouch, the mapmaker chewed, distaste showing plainly on his face. Moments later he used the cup of water to help him swallow the stuff.

"'Tis one of Charlotte's remedies to ease the pain," he explained, carefully lying back again. "There's work to be done, Peter. The horses have to be seen to and more wood has to be gathered for the fire. When you're done with that, I'd be pleased to have some dry trousers."

Grateful that he had been given something to do, Peter left to attend to the horses and then to gather dry clothing for both Thompson and himself. He returned to the fire to find that the explorer had fallen into a deep sleep that lasted for more than an hour. When he awoke, to Peter's great relief, he was able to sit up straight and say, "Well then, lad, whilst I make some plans, suppose you make tea."

CHAPTER 6

Peter slept badly the next couple of nights, jumping at every rustle in the dry brush made by the night creatures of the forest. When Thompson finally told him he had to leave and set out on his own to get help, he wanted to protest, but he knew he mustn't. Thompson was right. Although the explorer's leg didn't appear to be broken, it was greatly swollen and he couldn't ride. It had taken two days to fashion a shelter of pine branches and dried grass and to collect a large heap of wood for fires. Now Thompson was able to hop around with the aid of a forked branch from a bare cottonwood tree and did all he could to help Peter prepare for his lonely journey.

It was still dark when, on the third day, Peter rose and kindled the fire, trying not to wake his sleeping companion. But Thompson stirred and thrust his head out of his shelter. "'Tis time then, is it?" Slowly, he emerged, dragging his musket with him. Handing the weapon to Peter, he said, "You have game enough to last you on your journey and likely won't have need of this. Take it nevertheless. I have my two long pistols to keep me company."

Peter nodded wordlessly, remembering how he had

lost his own musket. He listened carefully as Thompson cautioned him not to hurry so fast that he forgot to rest the horses. “It’s of great importance that you don’t stray from this water.” He gestured to the nearby river. “I’m certain now that it’s the Brazeau and that it will lead you to the North Saskatchewan. When you reach it, follow it upstream until you arrive at the fort and stay there until Alexander Henry comes from Whitemud House.”

“This might take a long time.”

The explorer’s reply was terse. “Aye,” he said, clapping Peter on the shoulder once, then turning back to his shelter.

Peter’s progress in the forest was slow, and his arms ached from the continuous tugging of the two packhorses that seemed to find it impossible to travel in step. But each time he felt fear or despair creeping into his weary body, he pushed it away with thoughts of Thompson lying alone and in pain. He told himself it was up to him now to do his best to get help.

Peter quickly became irritated with the river he was following. Fed by rivulets of smaller streams, it had widened considerably as the hours passed, and its course snaked downward through dense stands of tall, rough-barked trees, making it impossible to tell how far he was still from the North Saskatchewan. When ahead he noted a thinning of the trees, his mood brightened. As he urged his horse forward, he cautioned himself not to set his hopes too high. When he finally emerged from the trees, he found himself at the top of a long, low hill covered by dead grass and clumps of brush. There, at the bottom of the hill, was the North Saskatchewan winding through the prairie. Peter rubbed his eyes in disbelief.

He was almost certain he also spied four canoes heading upstream. Positive now, he wondered if they were hostile Peigans. But, no, Thompson had told him that Peigans didn't use canoes. They rode horses. Peter swallowed hard. Could it be the brigade? His heart pounded madly as he gathered his reins. They were coming fast. He had to hurry if he wanted to intercept them.

Behind him the sun had already dipped below the tips of the tallest foothills, and the long shadows cast by the occasional spruce or cottonwood disguised the hollows in the soil, making the race down the slope doubly perilous. He slowed his mount once, thinking to halt and load his musket so he could signal the brigade, then almost immediately kicked his horse into a gallop once more. A shot from his gun might bring trouble again. Peter's mount stumbled twice and almost fell, but he didn't try to slacken her speed until they were in shouting distance of the great river.

When he reached the North Saskatchewan, he slid off his sweating horse and led her and the pack animals down a shallow ravine to the river to allow them to drink. Already the canoes had approached the mouth of the Brazeau and were sweeping past its turbulent entrance to angle to the shore where Peter waited. He greeted the men, trying not to show his disappointment. They weren't part of the missing brigade.

There was one man he did know — tall, lanky William Henry, cousin of Alexander Henry of Whitemud House. It was William who had brought the boats from the east with provisions for Thompson's journey through the mountains. Upon seeing the man, Peter was so relieved that he had to struggle to keep tears from his eyes.

William leaped from the boat and grasped Peter's shoulders. "What the devil are you doing here, and where are David and the hunters?"

Stumbling over his words, Peter presented the bare facts and would have given the details had not William turned to the waiting men and ordered them to build a fire to cook some of the meat on the packhorses.

"They haven't seen a chunk of meat for three days," he said to Peter. "Now let's find a comfortable rock and I'll hear the rest of your tale."

When Peter finished speaking, William was silent for a long moment before he stood and said, "Plainly, David must be attended to, though nothing can be done until the day breaks. Then I'll take your horses and one man to find him, and you must go on with the boats to Rocky Mountain House. My cousin will have arrived there by now, since he and the others rode cross-country. He must be told of David's missing men." William rose then and motioned for Peter to follow. "I'm ready for a strip of that elk meat. We've had nothing but pemmican for three days."

"Elk?" Peter glanced at the fire where the men were cutting meat from one of the carcasses they had taken from the pack animals.

"Most call them red deer," William explained. "I did, as well, until I spoke with a gentleman from New York who's an expert in these matters. He identified the beast as an elk, not a deer."

As Peter filed this bit of information in his head to tell Thompson later, he felt a rush of concern for the wounded man and suddenly something else — almost affection for the solemn, taciturn explorer. "Mr. Henry, couldn't one of your men take a message to your cousin and I could go with you to find Mr. Thompson?"

William halted abruptly and peered at Peter for a long moment, then said, "No, and for many reasons, Peter. First, my cousin will have a hundred questions to ask of you that one of my men wouldn't be able to answer, and second, you have the look of one who has travelled far enough for now astride a horse. You'll do well to sleep when you can in the canoe to prepare you for what comes next."

"Yes, sir," Peter mumbled, knowing full well he shouldn't argue with a chief trader.

William chuckled, and as he continued to walk to the fire, he said, "And you need feel only a little concern for David. I've no doubt he has his Bible to read and his journal to add words to when he wishes. The time will pass."

Peter shook his head. "He gave it to me with instructions to write details of my journey to the North Saskatchewan."

William turned and stared at Peter. "'Tis odd he would part with the thing unless he feared —" He stopped himself and instead said, "I expect you had little time for writing."

Peter grinned. "I best get to it now before it's too dark to see."

The meat had been taken from the packhorses, but the pouches still hung on each side of the animals as they grazed. Recalling that Thompson had put his journal in a pouch by itself and strapped it on the horse with the black mane and tail, Peter approached it first. His breath caught in his throat when he saw that the strap that kept the pouch closed had broken. With shaking hands he lifted the flap and felt inside. It was empty! Hoping when there was no hope, he dug frantically in the pouch on the other side and in the ones hanging from the second packhorse. Although they weren't empty, none held Thompson's precious journal.

Peter's perch on the bales of trade goods the canoe carried was far from comfortable, but he slept most of the two days it took for the four canoes to reach the end of their journey. It was the shouts of welcome and the grinding sound of the bow of the canoe scraping on the shore that awakened him with a start. On a hill overlooking the river loomed the tall stockade of Rocky Mountain House. Peter leaped from the canoe into water up to his knees and shook his head to clear it of sleep. A voice shouted his name, and Alexander Henry emerged through the fort gate to stand, fists on hips, looking down at him.

"Peter, what in the name of all that's holy are you doing here? And, may I ask, where's David Thompson? The men of his brigade would be interested in learning that, as well."

"Where are they?" Peter asked eagerly, scrambling up the zigzag path. "We tried to find them."

"You first, lad," Alexander demanded. "They're safe as far as I know. Now where's David, or has he lost you, too?"

The words tumbled from Peter's mouth as he explained the difficulties they had encountered in the last fortnight. He omitted the fact that they had been lost.

Alexander bore little resemblance to his cousin. While William was clean-shaven, Alexander wore a neatly trimmed beard, and though they were the same height, Alexander was heavy-set. But their greatest difference lay in their manner. William was quiet and calm, and Alexander greeted every situation with loud words interspersed with a few choice curses.

When Peter finished his story, Alexander clapped himself on the forehead. "This is worse than I thought. You mean to say our esteemed mapmaker, Mr. David Thompson, now wants his brigade to meet him downriver at the Brazeau?"

Peter swallowed hard, but he spoke firmly. "Mr. Thompson believes it's the only way. He said to tell you that blood was spilt when the brigade tried to go up the North Saskatchewan. Do you know where they are?"

"Aye, that I do know." Alexander spat on the ground. "The entire lot, including three of their Cree wives, were here when I arrived two days ago. They said the Peigans stopped them about forty miles upriver and had a bit of a skirmish, though there was little damage to either side, except for one of ours who bumped his big nose on a rock. The Peigans made them return to this post, for they'll allow no one to travel upriver to trade with the Kootenays. I, in my infinite wisdom, outfoxed them by giving them enough rum for a sleep sound enough to allow the canoes to slip away upriver. Clever, I was."

"When they woke up, did they wonder where the brigade was?"

Alexander laughed without mirth. "In the morning

when they woke with aching heads, I told them the canoes had returned downstream to Boggy Hall."

Peter closed his eyes, not even wanting to think of a way to connect the brigade with Thompson now unless someone found the men and turned them back. But the Peigans might be furious when they learned Alexander Henry had tricked them. And there would be Bercier with the horses waiting at the mouth of the Brazeau. What a mix-up! There was nothing that could be done, though, but to return to Thompson somehow and allow him to sort it out.

However, Alexander already had a plan. "I suppose I could waste more rum so the brigade can slip past going downstream this time."

"Would that be possible?" Peter asked, hoping the man wasn't joking.

Alexander sighed deeply. "Oh, aye, I expect it is."

Before Alexander could turn away, Peter reached inside his shirt for the letter Thompson had given him and handed it to the chief trader, who read it hurriedly. When he finished, he said, "After we send the brigade on its way to David, I'll ride back to the Brazeau with you. He wishes for four horses and two dozen dogs to pull sleds, and I have a wish to do some hunting."

Although Peter was puzzled, having heard nothing of sleds, he made no comment. Instead, he cleared his throat and said, "There's something more, sir. The other Mr. Henry asked me to tell you that if Mr. Thompson still plans to go on across the mountains, he'd like to go with us. He very much would like to see the Pacific Ocean."

The chief trader shrugged, then nodded. "If that's

his wish, fine, though I hope he'll bear in mind that it isn't certain David Thompson will find this great river he seeks to lead him there. Both Alexander Mackenzie and Simon Fraser made the same effort and failed."

Peter kept silent, though Boulard had told him that both of those men had found rivers that led to the ocean, but they were too fierce for use as trade routes. His heart sank when it occurred to him that Thompson's Columbia River could be the same.

Chapter 7

Three more precious days passed before the return of the man who had ridden through the forest to intercept the brigade. "They say they'll be here tomorrow night," he reported.

Peter thought that sounded a bit hopeful, and Alexander Henry seemed to agree. "Aye," he said thoughtfully. "The river's running fast and they're going downstream." Then he said to the messenger, "Well done. And you didn't forget to tell them to wait well above the bend of the river until we give the signal?"

The man nodded, grinning. "Boulard first said since he isn't a cat it isn't possible for him to lead the canoes so far in the dark, though when he learned his friend David Thompson was in trouble he wished to return immediately."

"No surprise there." Turning to Peter, Alexander said, "I've given one of the men orders to catch the dogs David wants. You best see he picks the stoutest and pens them in with the horses. You'll need their strength to pull sleds when the snow becomes too deep for the horses."

If the snow's too deep for the horses, how will we get

through it? Peter wondered, though he said nothing. He followed the sounds of shrill yapping and deep-throated barks coming from the very back of the stockade. As he rounded the corner of the carpenter shed, he was astonished to see dozens of dogs darting in and out of a cloud of dust. In the middle of the confusion, holding a club, was the ugliest man Peter had ever seen. Before he could offer to help, the club swung, and with a cry of pain, a large, long-haired, black-and-white dog turned back at the man and bit him on the arm. His face contorted with rage, the voyageur raised the club again.

Peter cried out, "Don't!" as the heavy club crashed against the head of the animal. He watched in horror as the dog tried to stagger away, with the man following, club upraised to strike again. "Stop it!" Peter shouted, and this time the man paused and spun around.

The short-legged, bear-like man glared at Peter, and he shivered from the intensity of the dislike he saw on the scarred face. The moment was broken when the voyageur sneered and again raised his club over the stricken dog. Desperately, Peter darted forward and grabbed the man's arm, demanding again that he stop. The arm swung without effort, and Peter landed on the ground. He turned cold with fear when the voyageur moved toward him.

At that moment a voice called out, "Hey, DuNord, what are you doing?" Then three men emerged from the carpenter shop.

The voyageur replied by giving the men a contemptuous glance, then threw down his club and stalked away to the fort's gates. Looking at one another, the other men shrugged and returned to the carpenter shop, leaving Peter to deal with the dogs.

Peter knelt beside the unconscious animal. When he reached out to touch its head, matted now with drying blood, the world around him suddenly disappeared into a mist. Through the mist he saw the blurred figure of a man holding the limp body of a small black-and-white puppy.

His pulse racing, Peter tried to cling to the vision, but it faded almost as quickly as it had come when he heard a voice call his name. He turned to see Alexander Henry striding toward him.

"I see DuNord is back quarrelling with the rest of the men," the chief trader said. "Did he leave you to do —" He stopped speaking when he reached Peter's side and looked down at the dog. "I expect this is his work. I best get my gun and shoot the poor beast."

Peter sprang to his feet. "No, please don't. I can take care of her." He pointed at the stricken dog. "See, sir, her eyes are open now."

"You want this one for yourself then?" Alexander asked. When Peter nodded, he added, "I had an animal such as this one myself back in the old country. She was a grand friend." As he turned away, he called over his shoulder, "Look after her then, but first get some dried fish and persuade the dogs you'll need into the corral."

The dog struggled feebly as Peter half carried, half dragged it into the empty guard post in a corner of the fort. Closing the door and propping it shut with a stick, he raced to the dark wooden shed where barrels of dried fish and dried buffalo stood side by side.

Although most of the dogs were more than half-wild, in less than an hour Peter was able to use the tantalizing odour of dried fish to coax twenty of them into the corral. The moment he finished he sped back to the guard post. Cautiously, he opened the door and leaped back as a snarling ball of fury rushed past him and disappeared through the gates of the fort.

Disconsolately, Peter walked to the front of the buildings where Alexander was outlining his plan for reuniting Thompson and his brigade. "Word has been sent to tell them they must return very silently and pass by to meet David at the Brazeau."

There was a murmur of surprise, and Alexander put up one hand. "I'll explain why this is so later, but we have a more important matter to discuss right now." He looked at each of his men. "The Peigans aren't so easily deceived, and they may be suspicious if we offer them generous drinks of rum again. Who will say they were recently wed and that we're celebrating?"

"Moi!" a voice called out. "For a cup of rum I will marry as many times as you wish."

"Ah," Alexander said, "I wouldn't wish so much trouble for you, Boudreau. Instead we'll ask them to join us on the occasion of your name day."

There was a roar of approval.

With a feeling of concern Peter moved through the open gates of the fort and saw that across the river the trees were casting long shadows. The wounded dog would be fair prey for the prairie wolves that often howled throughout the night. Although he had little hope, he knew he had to make an effort to find her.

For a hundred feet the trees had been cleared around the stockade, but waist-high dry brush stabbed at his clothing as he moved slowly around the fort. He wouldn't have spotted the dog had not a last ray from the setting sun shot squarely on her. Her lip curled and she gave a throaty growl. Not wanting to frighten the wounded animal, Peter backed away. Then, realizing he still carried the packet of dried fish he had meant to give to her earlier, he pulled it from the pocket of his jacket and moved forward slowly. From a dozen feet away he paused and dangled the fish from his hand. The dog's nose twitched as she sniffed the slight breeze that sent the fishy aroma in her direction. When, with obvious disinterest, she glanced away, Peter tried again and again to offer her the fish. However, he failed even to get a nose twitch in response. Thinking she was too hurt to have an appetite, he retreated and decided to get water for her.

Sprinting back to the gate doors, Peter almost collided with Alexander. The chief trader interrupted his stammered attempt to apologize by asking, "How are you faring with the dog?"

"When I tried to give her some fish, she ran clear out of the fort. I'm thinking she might want some water."

Alexander stroked his chin. "There are some that can't bear the smell of the dried fish and prefer to hunt rabbits for themselves. Try her on a bit of the buffalo hanging in the shed."

With a grin of thanks Peter raced around the trade rooms and slipped into the dark shed. After a few quick strokes of his knife, he had a half-dozen strips of buffalo. Again, using the breeze to prove he had something better than fish, Peter approached to within six feet of the dog before she leaped to her feet and growled. Taking one step backward, he tossed a strip of meat and she caught it before it hit the ground. Encouraged, he moved forward one step and tossed a second piece, which she caught as easily as the first. But after swallowing it, she growled a warning. This time Peter stood his ground and waited for a moment before he took another step and placed the clay bowl of water under a bush. He backed away, but she ignored the water and watched him.

"You have to come inside," he said softly. "It'll soon be dark and the gates will close." He waved another strip of buffalo and retreated to the end of the stockade. His heart leaped when the wary animal followed. After tossing a fourth piece of meat, he moved around the corner almost to the gates. Holding his breath, he waited and let it out only when her head appeared. With the aid of the remaining two strips of buffalo, he managed to get the dog into the fort and behind the trade rooms. With no more strips of meat to offer her, Peter could only hope she wouldn't run through the gates again. And she didn't. After waiting expectantly for meat that didn't appear, the dog turned away from Peter, found a space between the corral and the carpenter shop, and curled up to sleep.

In the morning when Peter found the dog, he put out his hand and she backed away with a growl. He spent the entire day coaxing her to accept him with frequent bribes of meat. By the end of the day, she stopped growling at his approach and would snatch meat from his hand. One more day and perhaps he would be able to touch her, he hoped.

By midmorning the next day, Peter had given the mistrustful canine the simple name of Dog. Later that same day he learned there would be scant time for making friends with Dog when Alexander said that by now the brigade should be close enough to slip past Rocky Mountain House during the night if the Peigans didn't see the voyageurs.

If Peter wanted to take Dog with him, he knew he had to work fast. He searched a pile of discarded harnesses in the back of the fort and found a thin piece of leather long enough for him to fashion a loop on the end. With it held behind him in one hand and strips of meat in the other, he went in search of Dog.

Peter found the animal sleeping in the sun behind the fort walls, and though he approached silently, she was on her feet and backing away from him before he could throw the loop over her head. He slid to the ground, leaned his head against the stockade, and closed his eyes. "I don't have time for foolish games," he muttered softly. "When I leave here, there will be no more meat for you. It will be only fish, fish, and fish."

A plaintive whine, so muted he first thought he had imagined it, startled Peter, and he opened his eyes to discover that Dog had wriggled closer. With a feeling of delight he carefully put out his hand. Instantly, she backed away.

Peter rose to his feet and sighed as he looked at the animal. "Too bad. If I had more time, we might have become friends."

When he gathered up his strap and turned to leave, his way was blocked by a figure that appeared around the corner of the building. DuNord stared at him, eyes filled with scorn, yellow teeth bared with his sneer. "That one," the hulking man said, gesturing at Dog, "she is a bad one. I will not see the animal live who bites DuNord."

Peter whirled to see where Dog was, but she had disappeared. Furious, he sputtered, "You ... you ... you just leave that dog alone. Mr. Henry —"

Before he could finish, DuNord made a sudden jump toward him. Instinctively, Peter fled around the building to the safety of the front part of the fort where busy men were working. DuNord's laughter followed him.

CHAPTER 8

They started later than Peter had hoped, making it necessary to camp two nights before reaching the Brazeau River. To save time, instead of following the river they cut across the prairie, and it became too dark to find their way through the new growth of poplar and fir trees that thrust their way up through the charred remains of an old forest. Back at Rocky Mountain House he had tried not to be concerned about David Thompson, but when the wind whistled around the fort at night he wasn't able to keep his thoughts from the dark and lonely woods where he had left the explorer. He hoped mightily that William Henry had found Thompson.

For Peter the journey had begun badly. He hadn't given it a second thought when Alexander Henry had announced he was taking three men to hunt with him on his return from taking dogs and horses to Thompson. He wasn't surprised when most of the men in the fort volunteered to go, for he already knew how much the voyageurs loved to hunt. When he found that one of the men chosen was DuNord, he had no fear that the man would trouble him with Alexander nearby. His worry was for Dog when later DuNord returned to Rocky Mountain House. She had refused to be caught and tied with the other dogs so they could be led away from the comfort of the fort. When he rode away, Peter had glanced back and spotted her sitting in front of the fort, looking after them.

That night it was with a heavy heart that he helped unload the packhorses and took them to water and then fed the tired dogs. Alexander had said they could be turned loose the next day without fear of them returning to the fort. By the time he finished with his chores, the smell of cooking meat reminded Peter how hungry he was himself, but first he turned upstream for a quick wash. Then he halted suddenly. In the light of the autumn moon he saw what appeared to be a wolf lapping water a short distance away. It couldn't be one of the dogs. They were still tied and noisily eating dried fish not far behind him.

The stiff, damp breeze icing his face told Peter the animal wouldn't catch his scent, and he slipped behind a short, thick bush to watch. The animal finished taking water and turned to examine its surroundings. Crouching low, it began to creep toward the smell of cooking meat. Peter's heart leaped in delight. It was Dog!

His first impulse was to jump up and greet her, but instinct cautioned him to stay hidden. He watched as she crept to the small clearing where his companions were seated on logs chewing their supper. She was hungry. Peter moved backwards to where the horses pawed at the wet ground as they searched for feed. Straightening then, he stepped into the light of the fire, chose a tin plate, took a full ladle of meat, and helped himself to a half-dozen of the rock-hard biscuits made by Alexander himself.

The chief trader's eyebrows shot up. "Whoa, lad! I'm glad you appreciate my cooking, but I was hoping to have some left for the morning."

Peter felt every eye upon him, and his face grew warm. "I ... I didn't know. I'll put some back."

Alexander laughed. "Oh, go away with you. I was only teasing you. There's plenty more."

Peter returned to the shadows and found a flat rock for a seat. He chewed the meat — disappointed it was buffalo again. Peter preferred deer or rabbit. He finished a strip of meat and a biscuit, then rose and called out, "I'm going for water."

Alexander stood also. "And I'm about to have a last pipe before I bid good-night to the world."

Dog had left her position at the edge of the bushes and disappeared. Knowing her taste for buffalo, Peter slowly waved a chunk of it in the air as he turned in a full circle. The wind will carry the scent, and she must be starved. He was right. As he completed his circle, he heard a faint sound, and Dog appeared only a few feet away.

"Come along, Dog," he whispered, dangling the meat from his fingers as he crouched close to the ground. "Come along."

Hoping Dog would creep near enough to touch, Peter was startled by the flash of black and white that streaked by him. The meat disappeared. He heard a chuckle nearby and turned to find Alexander leaning against a slim poplar tree. "It occurred to me it was a bit odd you fell in love with my biscuits. No one else has."

To cover his embarrassment Peter said, "I do like them." He gestured in the direction Dog had fled. "She must be terribly hungry following us all day."

"And she'll no doubt follow again tomorrow now that she knows she'll be fed." Alexander turned back toward the fire and spoke over his shoulder. "Best leave the rest where she can find it and get to your bed. Sun-up will come soon enough."

They travelled northwest, guided by the weak rays of a sun that appeared infrequently, until they emerged from a particularly dense part of the woods onto a bluff and saw the North Saskatchewan threading its way below. In the distance water tumbled down to meet it.

"That's the Brazeau, for sure," Peter said. He turned in his saddle to survey the river as far as he could.

There was no sign of Thompson, but Alexander spotted a thin wisp of smoke coming from a bluff where the river rounded a bend. "Let's hope that's either David or the boats. I've no wish to begin a hunt for him or for them."

The smoke was coming from a campfire, and the men of the canoe brigade were sitting around it drying their clothes. Peter saw with happy relief that Thompson was able to jump to his feet and call out a greeting with the rest of the men as the riders approached.

Peter felt a glow of pleasure when Thompson said, "Well done, lad," before he passed by him to greet Alexander. Thompson reached up to shake the hand of the chief trader. "The men told me of your ruse to get them past the Peigans. I'm grateful for your expertise in deception."

"You're welcome, David," Alexander said as he swung

off his horse. "But I'm thinking your plan to follow the Athabasca River into the mountains is foolhardy. Man, winter's near upon us! You'll never get through."

Peter saw Thompson's face change as he led the chief trader back to the fire. His square chin was set in a familiar stubborn way, though he spoke quietly enough. "I must go *now*, Alexander. This will be my last effort to find the Columbia and a safe passage to the Pacific. Who knows what may happen if I delay until spring?" He shook his head. "Both my head and my heart tell me I must go now."

"But, man, you've already made it possible for the company to trade west of the mountains," Alexander protested. "Isn't it enough that you have three posts there now?"

Peter knew how the mapmaker would answer that question. He had talked of it often enough. The company planned to send one of their ships around to the western edge of the country to where the big river emptied into the ocean. They would collect the furs brought down from the trading posts and take them to China where they could be sold for a large profit.

When Thompson finished explaining, Alexander shook his head. "'Tis naught but nonsense. You know the British Parliament would never agree. They promised exclusive rights to the East India Company to trade with the Chinese."

This time Thompson's mouth relaxed in a slight smile. "However, our lacklustre Parliament can't dictate to the Americans, who are free to trade wherever they choose." He strode over to his black iron instrument case lying under a tree and extracted a paper. Presenting it to Alexander, he said, "This is an agreement to allow our North West Company to purchase one share of John Jacob Astor's Pacific Fur Company. Under his banner we can ship our furs to China."

Alexander's face wore a frown as he read, and his tone was skeptical. "I hadn't heard that Astor agreed to this."

Thompson shrugged, and with a perfectly straight face said, "If the ship he sent around to the mouth of the Columbia arrives before we do, this paper should forestall any attempt they may make to keep us from trading there."

"David," Alexander said with an exaggerated effort to appear shocked, "I can't believe my ears. The most honest, truthful, Bible-reading mapmaker in the North West Company is planning to deceive the men of the Pacific Fur Company by pretending we're partners with them?"

"You mean the only mapmaker in the North West Company now that Mackenzie and Fraser no longer explore," Thompson said dryly. "Believe what you will. This has been planned, and I haven't been specifically told the two companies haven't agreed, so I may assume I'm right in thinking we're partners with them."

Alexander chuckled and clapped Thompson on the shoulder. "You're a good man for the company, David. Now what delicacies do you have for our supper?"

Spying Vallade, Peter anxiously inquired as to the whereabouts of Boulard, only to be told his friend was gathering more wood for the fire. Peter dismounted then and peered down the trail they had made through the brush. The dogs had been released that morning and had darted back and forth into the woods as they followed, but Dog had kept pace about twenty feet behind Peter. She sat quietly now and watched as he reached into his saddlebag and brought out the chunk of raw meat he had secreted there before they had started in the morning. When he held it out in front of him and began to walk toward her, she sat very still, and Peter thought her tail twitched slightly. Heartened, he moved again, and suddenly she leaped up, head down and hair standing along her spine as she bared her teeth.

A voice spoke behind Peter. "That is a bad one."

Peter whirled to find DuNord glaring at Dog.

"You ... you don't know anything about her. She's ... she's only afraid."

"I know her," DuNord said, holding out one arm for Peter to see the clear marks of a set of teeth. "I mean to kill her."

"You ... you just try it!" Peter said, hating himself for not being able to control his stammer when he was frightened. "That's my ... my dog."

DuNord stepped close enough for Peter to smell his sweat-stained buckskins, but Peter refused to back away. As he stared at the menacing face, his heart pounded so loudly he was afraid the man could hear it. Expecting a blow any minute, Peter felt relief wash over him when he heard Boulard's voice.

"Peter, *mon ami*!" There was a pause, then Boulard asked, "Is there trouble here?"

DuNord stepped back quickly and stared stonily straight ahead. Looking from Peter to DuNord, Boulard repeated his question.

Peter hesitated. He knew Boulard had the authority

to make DuNord leave him alone, but this was his problem to handle. "No," he said finally. "We were just talking about my dog."

Chapter 9

Boulard stood, hands on hips and head cocked, as he regarded Peter. "Young Peter, it has been but a few months, but to me it seems you are much more a man than the boy I first saw in Montreal."

Peter felt his heart swell with pride. To cover his feelings he switched subjects and told Boulard about Dog. As he talked, the voyageur's head nodded with approval. When he finished, Boulard said, "Your friend is my friend, Peter, so we will consider Mademoiselle Dog to be part of our brigade." He held out his hand and took a step toward Dog, who lifted her lip and snarled. Embarrassed, Peter tried to explain, but Boulard interrupted. "It is all right, Peter. There are others who have the same feelings for me. Come to the fire and have supper when you have seen to her comfort."

Thompson had found all his precious instruments safe, including the compass, and again he waved away Peter's stammered apology for losing the journal. "I'm the one who placed it in the saddlebag. I may be able to recall much of what I wrote in it, and when there's time, we'll make another."

Peter felt a rush of gratitude and affection for the

explorer and wondered why some found him hard and stern. However, as the days passed, it was easy to see Thompson was growing impatient with the wait for Bercier and the horses, for he kept riding up the Brazeau into the forest to listen for them.

After resting their horses for two days, Alexander Henry and his hunters decided to return to Rocky Mountain House. Before he left he told Thompson, "Running more than twenty horses through a hundred miles of woodland can't be done in a few days, David. Likely, you'll have another month to wait for Bercier. You might think of coming back to the House."

Peter, who had been hunting rabbits with Boulard, returned to the campsite in time to bid the chief trader goodbye and was appalled when he noticed there were only two men with Alexander Henry. DuNord was leaning against a tree, ignoring his companions.

Boulard appeared to have noticed this, as well, for when Alexander and his hunters turned their horses to ride off, he moved closer to Thompson and murmured into his ear.

"What?" Thompson asked absently. "Oh, yes, DuNord. Alexander asked me to hire him to go with us. He doesn't get along well with some of the men at Rocky Mountain House, but he's an excellent hunter."

Alexander Henry was wrong. Driven by Bercier, his wife, and his two sons, as well as Young Joseph, the horses arrived three days later, and four days after that they were loaded with the provisions from the canoes. Peter marvelled at the bales of supplies the animals transported, for the canoes had carried bell-shaped leather tents and leather boots for each of Thompson's men from Boggy Hall as well as trade goods. It was late October when they began their diagonal northwest trek across the land between the Brazeau and the Athabasca Rivers. Bercier and his family had gone on to Rocky Mountain House, and now they were twenty men with twenty-eight horses plus the packhorses and dogs. There were three Cree wives, but no children.

The day before, Thompson had selected DuNord and three others, who had accepted the order happily, to go on ahead as hunters for food for that night. The two men who were chosen to clear a pathway through the heavy brush and fallen timber were far less pleased, as were the rest who led the packhorses. Peter was disappointed that Young Joseph wished to return to his people and had sent Thomas, another Iroquois, to guide in his place. Peter liked Young Joseph.

The dogs followed willingly now, freeing Peter to take short side trips in the hope of seeing a deer or an elk hiding in the bushes. Thus far most of the animals he sketched for Thompson were dead ones brought back by the hunters. Their trail snaked on a gradual upward slope through a forest scented by fir, spruce, and the damp earth. The trees were spread thinly, which might have made it easier for the horses had it not been for the windfalls of burned logs, the result of long-ago forest fires.

Few birds sang as the caravan passed, but often a squirrel scolded them and silent grey birds flew from branch to branch, watching. Peter sometimes felt uneasy when he surveyed his companions. The men were the usual crew of Indians and mixed bloods who sang and joked as they paddled long hours in canoes over miles of raging rivers upstream as well as down. Now, on horses that hopped over fallen trees and stumbled into leaf-covered depressions, they were silent except for the occasional curse when they were slapped in the face by prickly fir trees as they passed. It didn't help their mood when, after four days of wearying travel, David said grimly, "Thus far we've come only eighteen miles. We must increase our pace as well as not allow our horses to tire. From this point onward we'll dismount every two hours and lead them for half an hour."

The grumbling increased, but Thompson ignored it as well as the frayed tempers as they crossed and recrossed the stony-bottomed creeks that soaked their boots. Peter's respect and liking for Boulard continued to grow, for he remained cheerful as he trudged over the same ground and brushed away gnats and mosquitoes. Thompson was a different matter, however. As the days passed, it wasn't difficult to see that he was becoming openly impatient with the mishaps that occurred due to carelessness, the worst being the near loss of a badly loaded packhorse as they picked their way over a narrow trail of loose stones high above the Pembina River.

Although it surged and crashed against the walls that held it in, the river wasn't very wide. But the sharp rocks jutting along its edges and the steep incline leading to it forced them to follow a trail high above the water in search of a safe place to ford. Peter kept close watch on the trail as he led his horse and the packhorse that followed until he heard a cry and glanced back to see one of the men hanging on to the reins of a packhorse as it began to slide downward.

"Petain, let him go!" Thompson shouted. "Let him go!"

Already sliding over the edge himself, Petain clutched the reins of the horse and dug his heels into the loose soil. Man and beast made deep grooves in the earth as they slid toward the rocks.

Peter held his breath, unable to move when he saw that Thompson had followed the hapless pair and was sliding fast, unaware that Boulard and William Henry were shouting at him to catch the rope they had thrown. A moment later Thompson was out of sight. The silence that followed was broken only by the crashing sounds of the river.

Peter's body was rigid with fear until a small cheer rippled through the men standing on the hillside. He stood in his stirrups as high as he could and saw that the horse, lying on its side now, had come up against a stand of new-growth aspens so small he wouldn't have thought they would hold the struggling animal. But they did.

It took the rest of the afternoon to get the terrified beast on its feet and unload it to pass the goods up to waiting hands. Then, with the help of another horse, the trembling animal was pulled up the trail.

After Petain's narrow escape, they camped early, and the men were given a ration of rum. Peter used this opportunity to spend extra time with Dog. Even though she still wouldn't allow him to touch her, he sensed they were becoming friends, for she had begun to seek him out at the end of the day. Peter chose not to believe this was because she was looking for her nightly bit of meat.

He had become more certain of that when she started to sleep only a few feet away from him each night.

Although Dog followed, she stayed out of the circle of firelight when Peter joined Boulard and William Henry, who were sitting on a fallen log having a last pipe before sleeping. It took only a moment for him to realize they were talking about Thompson, who as usual was out somewhere taking sightings by the stars. Peter listened with curiosity, for he knew little about their leader.

"It is possible the company will reward him handsomely for finding this great river of the west," Boulard said. "But me, I know David. Completing his map is of the greatest importance to him for these many years."

William took his pipe from his mouth and regarded it carefully. "And I've no doubt he'll do so." He looked at Peter and smiled. "Some say our explorer is a very stubborn man, but others admire him for his strong character." He chuckled. "I was in Montreal when his first shipment of furs arrived from west of these mountains. In one pack were a half-dozen white pelts of mountain goats found only very high in the peaks. One of the company fools jeered at them and told David not to send useless pelts. It seems that when the furs reached London they were a great success. David has small patience with those who don't appreciate the dangers and hardships his men face, thus when he received orders to send as many goatskins as possible, he sent word back that finding them was too risky for his men and he would send no more. And he didn't. I find much to admire in David Thompson."

The two men puffed on their pipes in comfortable silence until Boulard spoke. "We have travelled many rivers together and have wintered at three Indian camps. He does not ask any man to do what he will not."

Thompson's brave effort to save Petain may have been the reason the men seemed to grumble less for a while, but by the time they finally reached the icy edges of the Athabasca River, a few seemed ready to quit. It was DuNord who complained the loudest and kept the others stirred up. "Foolish to cross the mountains in winter," he grumbled loudly as they unloaded the horses. And later around the campfire he mumbled, "No meat will we find up there for us. We will starve."

Thompson ignored the complaints for the next four days as they followed the ice along the river higher and higher into the mountains. Where it was smoothest, the footing for the horses was the most precarious, and one after another they slipped and fell, sometimes knocking the packs from their backs and sometimes their riders. Three packhorses broke their legs and had to be shot. And eaten.

Peter's heart sank when they stopped to camp on the fourth night, and Thomas, their guide, informed Thompson that horses would be useless on the trails ahead. In the morning Thompson ordered seven men and the three women to take most of the horses back to Rocky Mountain House. The men were to return with more provisions and the mail.

Appointing himself spokesman, DuNord planted

himself in front of Thompson and demanded to know if he expected canoe men to walk. Thompson looked him up and down slowly, then said, "Aye, and you'll do it along with a sled and the team of dogs. You're being paid well for this journey. Go forward or go back with the horses."

Something in Thompson's cold tone must have convinced DuNord that it was useless to argue. He stalked away and stretched out on his blankets.

Axes rang as a large campsite was cleared and the tents were fastened securely to the ground. To Peter the camp seemed permanent, but when he questioned William Henry, the man chuckled and shook his head. "You forget we have to make snowshoes so we can walk on the deep snow that lies in the passes, and we'll need sleds for the dogs to pull, as well."

Peter stared up at the formidable mountains already covered in white. In the distance a small avalanche hit the bottom of the valley. Its thunderous noise carried on the dry, cold air made it sound closer than it was. He shuddered. Glancing up at the mountains made him feel a bit breathless, and the sounds of the avalanche doubled the feeling.

The trees were stunted — pine as well as aspen and willow — which the men appreciated. It was easier to chop down a small tree than a large one, and once down, the tree was less troublesome to split. Boulard had gone into the woods to look for birch, and Peter was told to string the snowshoes cut from wood. When DuNord saw him doing this, he spat on the ground. "Women's work." But Peter didn't mind. It was a welcome change from plodding up the river valley.

Dog had become sleek and fit on the diet of meat and campfire bread that Peter managed to give to her at night. Each time he fed her he was rewarded with a tiny whine of thanks and a twitch of her tail, though she still leaped away if he tried to touch her. His companions had become interested in his efforts to tame Dog, and jokes about which — in the end — would be master and which would be pet travelled through the camp. Peter accepted the teasing with good humour. It was better to hear the men laugh than to hear them complain.

Toward the end of 1810, men, sleds, and dogs were lined single file on the ice along the edge of the Athabasca River. The noise of the protesting, excited dogs drowned the sounds of open water in the middle of the river as it smashed against the ice. Peter was driving two dogs pulling the sled just behind William Henry, who was in charge of this phase of the journey. Thompson, Boulard, and Thomas had gone ahead to mark the trail, and thus avoided the hour it took to hitch the dogs — two to a sled. Having run free all summer, they weren't anxious to repeat their work of last winter.

Peter had tried to coax Dog into a harness without success, and so earned a comment from DuNord. "Dog not work. When meat gone, she roast over campfire." Then he laughed uproariously.

Peter had busied himself braiding strips of deer hide for harnesses and pretended not to hear, but his heart missed a beat. He knew eating dogs was quite common. But his dog was different; no one was going to eat her.

Sometimes Peter led his dogs, but more often he was behind the roughly built sled, helping them by pushing when they had to plough through a drift of snow. Each night when the sun dropped behind the hills ahead, he was so tired that he had difficulty unharnessing his dogs and often wished he could do as they did — curl up and go to sleep. There were chores to do, however, and he knew he wasn't the only one who was exhausted.

Without being told, he searched in the nearby trees for wood. Boulard joined him, and together they dragged a dried log to the centre of a small clearing. With the help of a few smaller pieces of tree and brush as tinder, the dry wood blazed into a welcome fire. Striding to his horse, Thompson removed the small keg from behind his saddle, and the men quickly gathered around him with their cups to receive a ration of rum. Thompson took none, nor did he offer any to Peter. Instead, he found his kettle and held it outstretched. Peter was meant to get water for tea.

Warmed by the tea and a generous helping of deer meat, Peter felt better. After feeding Dog and the sled dogs, he joined Boulard, who was standing close to the blazing fire. Seated on a nearby log, Thompson was speaking to William Henry. "I won't order you to stay, William, but it would please me if you agree. The dogs can no longer pull these heavy loads, and here would be a good place to build a depot to cache some of the goods until we need them. Two of the men will stay on with you to help add to your post."

Disappointment showed plainly on William's face, and for a moment he didn't reply. Finally, he said, "I'll do what's needed, though my hope had been to go on to the ocean."

Staring into the fire, Thompson nodded. "I understand, and in your place I'd feel the same. Wintering here will be a lonely business, but I need a man I can trust." With one hand he gestured toward the men moving about the camp. "All are good men, but some have no liking for this expedition, and I fear, without supervision, any I assigned to this post would return to the east and more than likely take the supplies with them."

As he listened, Peter found himself hoping DuNord would be one of the men to stay here at the river's headwaters, but then he chastised himself. William was his friend, and he didn't really wish him to be shut up all winter with DuNord.

CHAPTER 10

It took three weeks to construct a rough log shelter for William Henry, his two men, and the trade goods. Peter worked hard — sometimes driving the horse that dragged the long, unpeeled logs cut from tall lodgepole pines, sometimes braiding more snowshoes. Although everyone was tired by nightfall, the men seemed content to sit beside the fire and hear Thompson read aloud from his Bible. Later, one evening when the talk became more general, a voyageur named Fortrand looked at Thompson and bluntly asked, "*Monsieur*, from where did you come before here?"

For a long moment the explorer stared into the fire and didn't reply. When he did, Peter felt a wave of uneasiness, for Thompson's voice more than his words told how much he missed his own country. "I was born in London and there attended school. Each day I passed by an old and beautiful cathedral famous for its gardens of flowers in the summer. I'd stop to listen to the choir singing and sometimes had to run as fast as I could so I wasn't late for school."

Boulard chuckled. "In this London you did not hunt for your food, I think, nor make your bed in the snow."

Thompson smiled and shook his head.

"Did you ..." another voyageur began.

Thompson, however, stood and again shook his head. "Enough of memories. I must take one more sighting, and daybreak will soon be upon us."

Reluctantly, Peter rose from his seat by the fire. He wanted to hear more, for he had never thought of Thompson nor any of the men as boys like himself who also had to learn to shoot a musket and sleep in the snow.

In the morning Peter heard Thompson tell Boulard that he didn't fault William Henry for not choosing DuNord to stay and help build a larger post. "William feared the fellow's complaints would encourage the other man to do the same, and by spring all three would be ready for bedlam."

Boulard shrugged. "Monsieur DuNord may be of better material than it appears. Perhaps he will demonstrate he is a man as we cross these mountains."

They left the newly built post at the end of December, with the dogs pulling eight sleds of trade goods and baggage, and their last four horses carrying fresh meat and supplies of fat and flour. It was a bitterly cold day, but there was no wind and the sun was shining. Peter's spirits lifted when the men began to sing as, with one sled following another, they left the tiny post. It was a good beginning. However, after the first few days of trying to control the unruly dogs pulling the sleds, the enthusiasm dimmed noticeably and the men started to take two to three hours to get moving each morning while demanding to camp each day before sundown. Thompson ignored their complaints until DuNord pushed him too far.

Day after day the line of men had trudged upward with sleds overturning every time they struck a stump or a log hidden under the snow. On the ninth day, DuNord, in a fit of temper, threw his sled down the hillside with his dogs still attached. Packs of provisions flew as the sled broke along the way.

Thompson had been far ahead of the line and didn't learn of the commotion until Boulard sent a man ahead to call to him. When he returned, he glanced from the sled to DuNord, who stared back insolently. Quietly, Thompson said, "It needs a man of courage to cross these mountains. Not all are capable. You may take a double pack for yourself to carry and reload all else on the other sleds, or I'll give you a share of the supplies and you can return to Rocky Mountain House."

DuNord's bushy black eyebrows shot almost to his hairline in surprise. "You cannot. Alone, I would not live."

"Most likely," Thompson said, "and thus far I haven't been the cause of any man's death. However, if it comes to a choice between you and the success of our undertaking, you must know what my choice would be."

DuNord hastily piled boxes on the remaining seven sleds, then picked up two heavy packs to carry himself. Whenever Peter glanced behind him, he felt a tiny bit of sympathy for DuNord. Powerful as the man was, he laboured mightily through the deep snow with his heavy burden, his mouth set in a grim line.

Thompson must have had these thoughts, as well, for after less than three hours, he was waiting when the train of sleds caught up with him. "You, DuNord, unload one of the packhorses and take another man with you to hunt. There are tracks of sheep and red deer aplenty. Dead ahead is Jasper Lake where we'll make camp. Keep moving due west through the woods and you'll find us."

To Boulard, Thompson said, "I find the complaints from some of the men irksome. Here they worry about snow barely above their knees but will happily spend a winter in Montreal, though it be ten feet deep there."

Boulard nodded. "And some try to ease their fear by beating the dogs, even those who do their best to pull the sleds."

"You should have said as much at once," Thompson said. "We have few enough dogs. They mustn't be bruised to make it more difficult for them to pull in the heavy snow. I'll no longer set my pace to be so far ahead that I may better know what is happening behind me."

Peter turned away to hide his joy when they camped that night and Thompson announced, "It's time to rest the dogs. We'll camp here two nights, and since the wind and cold are bitter, you'll have a cup of rum."

Instead of the usual cheer there were only murmurs of approval from the weary men. Peter knew how they felt. His fingers and toes were numb, he ached with exhaustion, and the sight of the forbidding, snowcapped mountains ahead guarding the valley filled him with dread. Some of his fatigue disappeared, however, when Thompson said to the men, "You've done well. You can see that we're now deep into the mountains. My hope is that we'll cross them within a few days, and on the other side it will be less cold."

DuNord and his companion were unsuccessful in

their attempt to find game, which didn't help his sour disposition. He turned away from the fire now with a look of suspicion. "*Monsieur*, you say 'hope.' Do you not know where we are?"

Thompson waved his hand in the direction of the guide who was sitting away from the fire on a huge snow-covered boulder. "Thomas knows, and I trust him to show the way."

Peter was uneasy. Only the night before Thompson had expressed for the first time some doubt in Thomas's ability to find his way through the mountains. "He's an honest man," he had said to Boulard. "Even though the Iroquois have been here for nearly ten years, he doesn't pretend to know every river. But we trust each other — I with my compass and Thomas with his instincts."

The ice-encrusted Athabasca had become increasingly shallow as they penetrated deeper into the mountains. Fed here in the summer by trickling streams, the river was spread widely now around the snow-covered sandy mounds that jutted up from the riverbed. With Dog at his heels Peter stumbled along behind the sled, hardly believing his eyes whenever he glimpsed the glittering glaciers in the distance. There was snow enough everywhere, but the vast fields of ice crouching on the gigantic mountains appeared to threaten the dog train as it intruded farther into the river valley. Even Thompson's calm assurance seemed to lessen each time he paused to survey another ice-choked stream connecting to the river they followed.

One night they camped early and found enough wood for a fire to burn all night. Thompson, as usual, left the camp to climb higher and take a sighting for his journal. Again one of the men found this behaviour strange.

"Here, by the warm fire, we have food and good talk, but our leader prefers the dark sky to our company."

DuNord's tone was angry. "He makes maps for other men to make this hellish journey."

Hot words sprang to Peter's lips, but Boulard spoke first. "He charts our journey to learn if it is easier and faster for trading than the old way up the Saskatchewan."

Peter found himself scowling when DuNord's fellow complainer, LeTendre, spat and said, "A good company man then, but not a friendly one."

Again it was Boulard who responded. "Monsieur Thompson works hard for the company." He turned to Peter. "Have you learned how he became a mapmaker?"

Staring into the fire, Peter shook his head. Boulard crossed his legs, clasped his hands on his knees, and began. "Me, I was at Fort Churchill on the cold Hudson Bay for two years when David arrived from England." He gestured toward Peter. "He was of the same age as this one is now and away from his family for the first time, but no one ever heard him complain. Even from me, who knew the winters there, came plenty of complaining, I tell you. The walls of the room with his bed were as mine — thick with ice — and he had to walk up and down the trade room to keep warm even while wearing all his clothes."

When Boulard paused to poke a stick into the fire and light his pipe, Peter became aware that the rest of the men had stopped muttering and were listening. Satisfied that his pipe was drawing well, Boulard continued. "The captain of a supply ship gave to our chief trader, Samuel

Hearne, a copy of the map made by Captain Cook. One day he showed it to us. David saw it was only the coasts of this land that had been mapped — nothing of the rivers and mountains and prairies. It is then that he made the promise — he would be the one to find these rivers and mountains and place them on that map."

Boulard paused again as if trying to remember, then said, "It is impossible for me to think of the name of the head clerk who found great amusement in this promise. He was a fellow full of himself. For this reason he was much upset when David found a mistake in his ledger. Thinking to even himself, he suggested that David greet an Indian warrior entering the trade room by shaking the man's hand. In this way David might gain a good customer for the company. Suspecting nothing, David did so, and the Chippewa leaped back and pulled out his knife. It was fortunate for David that I ran to the trade room when I heard the shouting. It was difficult for me to persuade the Chippewa that David did not know that offering his right hand was a sign he wished to fight."

Vallade nodded. "Our Monsieur Thompson, he might have been killed."

"Certainement," Boulard agreed. "It appears David gave this much thought, and that night he said to this clerk, 'I do not know what I did to deserve your wrath, but it should not be enough to get me killed. To even us, I will turn my backside to you now so you can kick it.'"

The listeners burst into laughter, including Peter. Boulard looked at him reprovingly. "Why do you laugh?" he asked with mock severity. "David received the kick, though after that they were friends."

"Me, I did not see Fort Churchill," one of the voyageurs said, "but I have heard it is a bad place."

Boulard nodded. "Cold it is for much of the year and bare of trees. And there are big white bears that are always hungry." He shuddered. "If in this world food could be found only at Fort Churchill, I would starve before I would go there."

CHAPTER 11

The next day Peter heard a shout and saw that ahead of him the sled of a voyageur named Côté was tipping and the man was in danger of losing his load. Peter halted his own team and ran ahead to help right the sled only to see his own sled fly past him as his dogs raced to fight with Côté's team.

As he helped untangle the yapping dogs, Côté spoke wearily. "Me, I believe it is not so much the difficulties of the trail that makes a night's rest so welcome. It is these foolish events."

Peter heartily agreed. A dozen times a day there were mishaps of one kind or another. Often a harness broke or a sled cracked on a rock or a dog rolled down a hill, and too often it was DuNord or one of his fellow complainers who made the others wait while they sat down to rest. Thompson was getting more impatient as the days went by, for the miles were passing slowly. Thus Peter's scalp prickled with anxiety when the two teams started again only to find Thompson had left the head of the dog train and was coming toward them rapidly on his snowshoes.

Instead of being angry with the delay Thompson waved at them and called out cheerfully, "Make haste! Ahead is a small river that interests me."

The river didn't appear small to Peter. It was about forty yards wide, though it appeared to be as shallow as the Athabasca they had been following for so many days that he had lost count.

"We rest here for two nights," Thompson announced. "Tomorrow Pareil and Côté may have better fortune hunting for meat. The rest of you will make camp, while Thomas and I follow this stream to see if it will allow us to pass between the fields of ice."

Filled with a new energy born from hope, Peter knew he couldn't wait until their return to learn if they had found a way through this everlasting ice and snow. "Please, sir, I'd like to go with you and Thomas."

Thompson appeared surprised, then almost pleased. "Of course, Peter, but the climb won't be easy."

Peter felt a stab of resentment, wondering if Thompson — blind in one eye and with a bad leg — thought of him as less able. As though he had heard Peter's thoughts, the mapmaker nodded and said, "We'll be glad of your company."

Hastily, Peter dropped a handful of pemmican at Dog's feet and swallowed one himself before turning to scramble behind Thomas over the slippery rocks guarding the side of the water. As they climbed higher, Peter tried not to think of how steep the return trip to the camp would be and instead listened to Thompson exclaim about the beauty of the sun setting behind the mountains. Peter made no comment, but he had to agree it was a sight to behold, one he would someday like to paint. The gold and red streaks of wispy clouds drifting above the peaks and the shafts of light darting between them like golden arrows of hope almost made him forget how cold his hands and feet were. Still, he sighed with relief when Thompson called a halt and pulled out his telescope.

In the distance Peter saw only the tips of more mountains and no sign of a river valley leading through them. He slumped to his knees, suddenly weak with fatigue and the realization that it could be weeks or maybe months before they found the river the mapmaker sought. If they ever did. Peter wanted nothing more at this moment than to lie in the snow and stay there forever.

His thoughts were shattered by Thompson's sudden announcement. The mapmaker's eyes shone as he collapsed his telescope and said, "I'm confident we're at the beginning of our last ascent in these mountains. Rum all around tonight."

It took longer to pick their way down the steep trail they had made. When they reached the camp, Peter neither received nor wanted any rum. He longed only for his bed by the fire. Thompson, however, was still bursting with enthusiasm.

"This river I found with my glass we'll call the Whirlpool," he explained while the men drank their rum. "It leads upward, but due west, whilst the Athabasca trickles from a great field of ice to the southwest."

"What is the beginning of the Whirlpool River?" Boulard asked. "Is it possible we must find our way across on the ice mountains?"

"I can't be certain of its source," Thompson said

with characteristic honesty. "If it does come from an ice field, we'll find a way around it."

In the morning Thomas announced it was time to leave the last three horses behind, for it would be impossible for them to climb through the deep snow that lay ahead, and even if they could, there would be no grass or brush for them to eat.

Thompson nodded reluctantly. "Had we not the two moose Pareil and Côté succeeded in bringing down, we would slaughter one of the horses for food. As it is, we have no means of carrying more meat." He shook his head, and Peter heard him mutter, "The poor creatures won't find anything to eat hereabouts, either."

The next day Thompson gave one of his rare speeches to the men. "The most wearying part of our journey is almost behind us. Today we begin the final trek up this stream, which I'm certain passes through the heights that divide this continent. I'm also certain that on the other side of these mountains lies the river we seek and plenty of wood nearby to build a canoe."

Most of the men cheered at the prospect of travelling once more by canoe, but Peter heard DuNord grumble to a fellow complainer, "This mapmaker leads us, and we must follow like dogs." He gestured toward the biggest mountain Peter had seen yet. It loomed just north of their campsite. The voyageurs had named it La Montagne de la Grand Traverse. "It serves as a warning," DuNord said. "There is more hardship to come. I do not like this."

In the weeks that followed Thompson took his turn behind a sled to help the struggling dogs as they climbed upward over endless rocks hiding beneath the snow. At night the snow was soft under their bedrolls, but the cold seeped through the tanned leather hides under their blankets to stiffen their muscles and make walking difficult the next morning.

Although the days were sunny for the most part, the air was bitterly cold. Then, after a week of sunlit travel, the sky darkened abruptly. Peter, only mildly curious, turned to look behind him. Above a deep grey mist that obscured the mountains a black cloud had blotted out the sun and was boiling toward him with incredible speed. Peter stood, transfixed. A harsh urgency in the voice that called to him over the sound of the rising wind broke the spell, and he sprang ahead to grasp the lead rope. Dragging his team and sled, he stumbled after Boulard, who waited beside a deep cleft in the mountainside. Inside the opening Thompson and the rest of the men were already tossing aside rocks to make room for their tents.

"Would ... that we had ... warning enough ... to gather deadwood ... to build a fire," the explorer said, his words coming between gasps for breath as he shoved a heavy boulder into a dry creek bed that wove through the gap in the mountain. "I fear ... this may last ... for some time."

Pausing for a moment, Thompson ordered Peter to gather the food from the sleds and store it in his tent. After he accomplished this task, Peter, with Dog beside him, plunged farther into the cleft to find Boulard and help him put up the tent.

The wind was less violent here, but though it was mid-afternoon the sky was as black as midnight without stars. An hour ago Peter had felt almost uncomfortably warm from the exertion of pushing his sled through the deep snow. Now he could feel the sweat in his boots icing his feet. He stopped suddenly, and a feeling of rage swept over him as he looked around at the dark figures working swiftly to prepare protection from the stinging cold. Rage, because he had been sure that after the weeks of cold, hunger, and fatigue, the journey would be easier now.

In a moment of absolute clarity, Peter knew this was the end. They were going to die here. And he didn't seem to care.

Then a solid figure appeared through the snow, almost bumping into Peter. "It's you then, lad," Thompson said, his voice muffled by the scarf half covering his face. "Pass the word that each man must take his animals into the tent with him while they sleep. The dogs will help keep them from freezing. I'll share a tent with you and Boulard." When Peter didn't respond, he peered more closely at the boy's face and then shook his shoulders roughly. "There's no time for fear, lad. Get yourself up ahead and help put up your tent."

With the aid of a shove from Thompson, Peter forced his legs forward to the flat spot where Boulard was struggling to keep the tent from blowing away before he could fasten it down with heavy rocks. Wordlessly and with practised motions, the two of them managed to set up their shelter.

"Sacré Marie!" Boulard said as he stripped off his coat and shook the snow outside. "In my travels I encounter many storms, but none so bad as this."

Peter, too, shed his coat, careful not to knock snow inside their tent as he shook it outside the door. Out of the wind and snow he felt better now — almost ashamed of his moment of panic. Even so, their lives depended on how long the storm lasted.

Sharing the tent with the dogs was surprisingly without difficulty. They seemed only too content to huddle closely together, leaving barely enough room for Peter and his companions to sit up. And at night, stretching out beside the three men, their warmth made sleep possible. Thus it lasted for three days.

On the fourth day they awoke to find the sun driving away the clouds. Even DuNord and his friends seemed more cheerful as they chewed strips of dried meat and washed them down with snow. There was no need to urge them to hurry as they packed the sleds and hitched the dogs.

Less than an hour after the line started to move once more, a Chinook wind began to blow — its warmth welcome at first, then creating a new problem. Their snowshoes as well as the sleds repeatedly stuck in the softened snow. They were above the timberline now, the sun turning the snow to a blinding white that forced Peter to squint most of the time and peer through his eyelashes. His shoulders and arms burned with the effort of keeping his sled from tipping from side to side as the yapping dogs slipped and slid and at other times half swam through the watery snow. Dog was always at his heels.

Peter was uncomfortably aware that a hundred feet behind him DuNord was lashing his dogs with a braided deer hide rope, cursing all the while. The noise made Peter's head ache. When shrieks of pain penetrated the racket, Peter stopped to rest his own team and glanced over his shoulder. DuNord had halted and, with his rope doubled, was systematically beating a howling dog cringing in the snow.

Even though the warmer air had brought the snow down to about three feet, it hindered Peter's effort to reach the enraged man in time to save the helpless animal. It was an eerie sight: The other dog was strangely silent as it sat in the reddened snow beside its dying comrade.

Peter stared in horror at the bloody carcass, then up at DuNord, who stood breathing heavily from his exertion. *"Salaud!"* Peter shouted in halting French. "You dirty skunk!"

DuNord's eyes narrowed, and he took a step toward Peter, his fists clenched. Too furious to be afraid, Peter braced himself and readied his own fists. From behind him a voice twice barked an order, and DuNord slowly lowered his hands. Boulard put a hand on Peter's shoulder and spun him around.

"Return to your sled, Peter," he said firmly. "Me, I will deal with this one. Go."

Peter trudged through the snow and waited without looking back. Dog sat by his feet, and for the first time allowed Peter to touch her. A few minutes passed and then Boulard returned. "You chose an evil one to call bad names, Peter, though myself I do not blame you. Take my sled that I may watch your back." Boulard glanced down at Dog. "This DuNord, he is short one dog now and demands the right to harness his sled to your friend."

Aghast, Peter stared at Boulard, too stunned to protest.

The voyageur smiled ruefully. "You are not amused,

and neither am I. Mademoiselle Dog is one of us. Never will she pull the sled of DuNord."

Peter blew out the breath he had been holding and grinned weakly. Without speaking he moved his team past Boulard's sled and ordered them to go quickly. They had fallen far behind the rest of the dog teams, and Peter was determined not to be forced to make camp that night with only Boulard and DuNord.

Without stopping to rest the tired animals, the three teams followed the trail made by their companions and found them camped above the river. Nearby, an enormous glacier glowed greenly with the last light of the setting sun.

Thompson had disappeared, but he returned moments after Peter and his companions reached the camp. In a voice deepened with satisfaction, he said, "By my calculation, tomorrow we'll begin our descent on the west side of these mountains."

Peter wasn't surprised that there were no cheers from the men. They still faced a grim journey, and some of them were now openly suspicious that Thompson hadn't travelled this way before. After making known his opinion of the mapmaker's ability to find his way, DuNord had another bit of information to add to the atmosphere of uneasiness.

"There is a tale of a monster in these mountains," he said darkly. "LeTendre, and me, we observe the signs this night."

Rising to his feet, Boulard yawned and stretched. "I have examined this big footprint you and LeTendre believe to be made by a monster. As for me, I believe it to be that of an old bear, and Monsieur Thompson agrees.

A very large bear, to be sure. But a monster? No."

The next morning Peter awoke damp and cold after a night of restless sleep broken by dreams of huge white bears creeping toward him while the men stood by laughing. Shaking off his dark mood, he reminded himself that the trail would be mostly downhill now and they would make better time. Before the morning was over, though, he learned how wrong he was.

They followed above the banks of a stream openly flowing westward. Thinking this must be the river Thompson sought, Peter was elated until Thomas said his people called it Wood River. If the mapmaker was disappointed, he didn't show it. Instead he grinned sourly. "I, David Thompson, by the authority of the king of England, do hereby rename these waters Flat Heart River in honour of the gloomy spirits of this company of explorers."

Peter observed that none of the men appeared to find their leader's remarks amusing.

Even though they were wallowing in increasingly deep, soft, wet snow, the dogs still managed to increase their speed when they went downhill, but too often found themselves on one side of a tree and the sled on the other. Entertaining though this was, time was wasted untangling the mess, and the air was filled with the whining and yelping from the dogs and the curses from the men. Peter stopped laughing at the antics of the dogs and started to worry as it became increasingly clear they couldn't continue to pull their heavy loads in the wet snow.

Scattered trees had begun to appear here and there, and when they neared a stand of thick white pines,

Thompson halted the train and announced they would relieve the dogs of some of their loads here. Boulard climbed partway up a tall pine to loop a deer hide rope over a heavy branch so that spare provisions could be hung until needed. Now, besides Thompson's metal box of instruments and papers, flour, fat, dried meat, and rice on the sleds, there were only tents and clothing for the men.

Even though the loads had been lightened, a few of the voyageurs continued to complain bitterly with each step and insisted on resting every half-mile. Then rain began to fall. Hunching his shoulders, Peter plodded onward at the edge of the water. He sighed as once more they had to cross the narrow stream zigzagging like a feather in a windstorm. Soaked and miserable, Peter paused on the other side while his team and Dog shook themselves free of water and watched Boulard lead his animals across.

"Not so much this," the voyageur said, wiping the drops from his eyes. He grinned crookedly. "*Mon père* wished for me to go to school to become a man of letters, but I, with the wisdom of a child, preferred to do this."

Knowing the doughty Boulard was half joking, Peter tried to think of how to reply in kind when his ears caught a faint rumble of thunder in the distance. Automatically, he peered upward, expecting to see lightning, as well. Instead he saw that a cloud of snow near the top of a mountain was rushing downward, burying the trees as it went. Bringing up the end of the train of sleds, DuNord had stopped to rest higher up on the trail they had made coming down the mountain.

"DuNord!" Peter screamed, startling Boulard

into whirling around. "DuNord, *vite*! *Vite!*" Without thinking Peter leaped back across the stream through water up to his knees, shouting as he went. Reaching the opposite bank, he raced up the hill, his heart pounding. Gasping for breath, he paused and pointed upward.

The rumbling had become thunder, and as he grasped the meaning of Peter's shouts, DuNord's eyes widened in terror. Leaving the sled and dog to fend for itself, he leaped down the trail, jumping and sliding. Freed, the dog raced ahead of him, the sled bouncing behind, and plunged into the river.

Boulard had followed halfway across the stream and caught Peter's arm now as he staggered back. Panting for breath, they clambered up the bank and crouched behind a giant cedar moments before a mass of snow, dirt, and rocks surged up the river valley.

Although the path of the slide was narrow, they were almost deafened by the roar as trees and earth tumbled less than a hundred feet from their shelter. When the noise died to an angry rumble, Peter yelled, "Did he make it? Is DuNord safe?"

Before Boulard could reply the man in question appeared, coughing and swiping with a rag at the dirt caked on his face. Without speaking he snatched the rope hanging from the harness of his sled dog and yanked it down the trail left by Thompson and the rest of the men.

Boulard shrugged. "This fellow, he appears to be safe, though he does not seem happy."

Peter's heart was still pounding, but he laughed when he realized he might have saved the life of the one person who wished to do him harm.

Following the water Thompson had named Flat Heart River, Peter felt a thrill of happiness when it led them to two others. One was small. Thompson called it the Canoe River, but the other was much wider. It must be the Columbia River!

Peter's joy disappeared when the mapmaker explained. "This one —" he indicated the larger river that the two smaller ones emptied into "— you can see flows northward, thus it is our old friend the Kootenay."

As the men stared, grim-faced, at the high walls of snow lining the Kootenay, Peter's spirits dropped into his boots. Sick at heart, Peter barely heard Thompson's words as he outlined their predicament. "You can see for yourselves," he said, gesturing to the banks of snow, "since there are few of us, it would be unwise to explore beyond the place where the three rivers become one until it's freed from much of the snow and ice. We have no knowledge of its current nor its direction. Here we can find our way up the Kootenay and wait in comfort at Rocky Mountain House for spring. There we'll find canoes for travel down to the ocean."

If Thompson had hoped mentioning canoes would make the voyageurs happier, he was disappointed. The angry muttering was louder than ever, and when the men started to journey along the shore of the snow, those that complained barely moved along its bank. Each was carrying little more than his own belongings now, for they had abandoned the sleds, and most of the dogs were making their own way in the woods. Dog, however, clung to Peter's heels.

That night Thompson disappeared, as usual, to find a clearing where he could see the stars well and returned while the men were holding strips of meat over the blazing fire and the flat bread was frying. He satisfied himself with a handful of pemmican and two rounds of the bread before beckoning to Boulard and Peter. "Come. We'll walk a little up this river and see what lies ahead for tomorrow."

When they paused to rest out of sight of the camp, Thompson said, "Your face tells all, Peter. I saw the look when I said this river was the Kootenay." Peter started to speak, but Thompson held up one hand. "Prepare yourselves for a surprise. I'm not certain, but I'm thinking this isn't the Kootenay and may be the Columbia we seek, though I prefer not to say as much in front of the other men."

It was easy to tell that Boulard was quite surprised. "But, David, how can this be? You believe this Columbia River you seek flows to the west. This one goes north."

Thompson nodded. "The same river on which we built Kootenay House in years past when we travelled the North Saskatchewan to get to Howse Pass and then made our way to this river, which begins in a big lake."

"I do not understand," Boulard said.

"Listen carefully," Thompson said. "With my glass I've seen that soon after the place where this river becomes one with the Canoe and Flat Heart Rivers, the waters turn south."

Obviously convinced, Boulard clapped Peter on the shoulder. "David, why do you not wish for the men to know? Why do we not hasten to build a canoe and go down this great river?"

"The water will rise, my friend, and the current will get stronger as the snow melts — perhaps too strong for this time of year. Thus we will continue to follow it to Kootenay House where we can find food, rest, and horses on which we can travel for part of our journey and thus avoid much of the floodwater."

If he hadn't been standing in deep snow, Peter thought he might have danced up and down, so happy was he that the end was almost in sight. Instead he grinned. "Let's go and see what's up ahead."

They didn't go far. Around the next bend they found an enormous rock jutting from the side of the mountain far into the water and creating a narrow passage filled with rushing water. Apparently undiscouraged, Thompson pulled off his knitted cap and ran his fingers through his chopped-off hair. "We'll have to build a raft and pole around this."

When they returned to the men who were trying to coax a flame from damp wood, Thompson explained the need for building a raft. Duloc, one of the worst of the complainers, jumped to his feet. "For me this is too much. It is madness to go on."

LeTendre followed suit. "I, too, will go back to the House. Who is with us?"

When the discussion was over, Peter realized that besides himself and Boulard there would be only six left to follow Thompson — Pareil, Villiard, Vallade, L'Amoureux, Côté, and Thomas, their guide. They would be too few now to make a raft and pole their way on a two-hundred-mile journey to Kootenay House.

Peter found he was right. Thompson decided to return to the camp where the three rivers met and winter there. The deserters came with them to the confluence of the three streams to receive their share of supplies. After they said their farewells, Thompson seemed more cheerful.

"They were useless as old women fearful of everything," the mapmaker said. "But that's the way with many men when they encounter the unfamiliar. The track of the creature in the mountains, the depth of the snow, and the avalanche and this impassable river are all too much for men who aren't strong."

Peter felt a glow of pride as he watched the weak men enter the trees. It wasn't too much for him, though, to be honest, there were times when he had thought otherwise. From now until they returned east of the mountains, he told himself, he would think only of today and not worry about tomorrow.

Reaching inside the pack he had dropped beside a tree, Peter pulled out a small rabbit that Thomas had helped trap the night before. Skinning it quickly, he whistled for Dog, thinking she had wandered into the forest to chase one of the black squirrels that raced up and down the trees scolding as they ran. Peter moved into the woods and whistled again. And again. He could no longer see the camp when he was startled by the sound of heavy footsteps in the trees behind him. Peter spun around and was paralyzed with fear. DuNord's face wore a grin that exposed broken teeth as he stalked toward Peter.

CHAPTER 12

When a rush of adrenaline overcame his fear, Peter glanced right and left. To try to circle around DuNord would be foolhardy, even though he might be able to outrun the heavy man. Somewhere to his left was the river — not a good choice. He tensed himself to dart deeper into the woods, then paused uncertainly. DuNord had stopped twenty feet away and was looking at him with a strange expression.

"I will do so no more," the hulking voyageur said. Puzzled, Peter waited, and DuNord repeated his words, adding, "I swore the oath. No more will I strike a dog."

Peter's mouth dropped open in surprise, and he stared back at the man.

DuNord gestured impatiently and frowned. "Many things in my life I have done, but never did I break the oath." With that he turned on his heel and trudged back through the trees.

Peter's mind whirled as he watched DuNord disappear into the forest. He wanted to call after him but didn't know what to say. Shaking his head, he thought about what had just happened.

Slowly, Peter retraced his steps to the camp where he

found Dog curled against a wide-branched pine tree in a soft pile of drifted snow. The campfire was sputtering, popping sparks onto the damp ground each time Boulard poked it with a stick. Thompson was leaning against a rock cleared of snow as he used his knife to scratch words on a piece of bark. Beside him stood Thomas, and nearby Villiard, Côté, and Pareil waited with heavy packs on their backs and straps around their heads. Peter felt a cold chill run up his spine. Were they leaving, too?

Thompson straightened and handed the strip of bark to Thomas. "Give this to William Henry and ask that he copy it on paper before he sends it on to Fort William." Then, to the waiting men, he said, "Take care through the pass if you choose to walk on the river. The ice might not bear your weight now. And take from the provisions we cached in the tree where we lightened the load for the dogs." Almost as an afterthought he added, "It's possible William Henry can't give you all the provisions we need. Please be sure to tell him we thank him for what he can spare."

Packs on their backs and leading the sleds they were ordered to leave with William, the men grinned as they waved and left the camp. Thompson looked at those who remained — Boulard, Vallade, L'Amoureux, and Peter. "It's now near the end of January. So we have about two months to wait for the snow to leave the river. We must first build a shelter and then find the means to build a canoe of sufficient size to carry men and goods. It will be a daunting task to find wood for the canoe. I walked a distance in these woods and found birch, but it appears the rind is too thin for our use. For shelter there is cedar aplenty, though the size of the trees may wear our axes down to the handles."

It was work enough to hack at the giant cedars to bring them down and split them into boards to line their shelter. The men had been skeptical when they first viewed the mighty cedar they were to cut down with two-pound axes. It was one of the smaller trees — about thirty-six inches in girth, but its branches reached to the sky. Working with a thin plank they had used to clear a place for the fire, Peter scraped away the four-foot-deep snow to make a large square beside the river. Then the men lined the sides and the floor with rough boards they managed to chop from the tree. More boards covered the top, and for the first time in five months Peter slept under a roof — one that leaked when the falling snow melted, but still a roof.

The last of the flour and fat had long since been eaten, but there was no lack of meat, for the deer survived by stamping the snow around patches of brush to nibble on all winter, thus creating a roofless shelter of their own. They were trapped in their shelters, making them easy targets.

Without success David and Boulard searched a wide area for birch trees with rind suitable for a canoe. The men seemed to be startled when Thompson proposed they build one by splitting cedar boards and lashing them together, but they set to work again hacking at a tall tree. Peter took his turn with the axe, and though his arms ached each night, he was glad to feel his muscles harden. He was happier still when — in mid-February — he heard Villiard cry a greeting and saw Pareil appear through the trees, followed by his companions who were leading a team of dogs pulling a loaded sled.

When the greetings were over, the sled was unloaded to reveal almost a hundred pounds of fat and plenty of gunpowder and lead, along with a bit of clothing material and three packs of trade goods. The men looked apologetic, and Villiard explained that William Henry had given all he could spare and had wished them Godspeed.

Thompson praised the men for their quick return and added, "The fat will go well when we cook the moose. They've been remarkably thin and their meat difficult to chew, and we can use some of that fat to make soap."

"And perhaps you brought a wife with you," Boulard said as he peered at the empty sled. "Who then is to cure the hides of these thin moose so we may braid it into ropes?"

Even Thompson laughed. It had been Boulard's task to dig pine tree roots from the frozen ground to use in lacing the boards together for the canoe, and he would have appreciated a length of sturdy rawhide to use instead.

Thompson no longer spent hours after dark searching the sky and writing in his new journal. Instead he worked beside the men, hacking and sawing. And, in spite of the strain on his one good eye, every night he read a chapter of the Bible by firelight. Peter liked hearing stories from the Bible, but he preferred the later hour when the talk became general. Often one of the men would tell of an experience he had had in the past. Villiard and Côté both had come from small farms not far from Montreal, and Pareil had once lost his britches escaping from a bear. Boulard, too, told stories of his youth, many involving *la femme*.

Thompson listened with apparent interest but volunteered nothing about himself until Pareil bluntly asked, "And you, Monsieur Thompson, how is it you left your country to live in this land?"

Peter held his breath, for he sensed the explorer didn't like to talk about himself. However, after thinking for a few moments, Thompson told the men what Peter already knew. The school he had attended in London had arranged for him to join the Hudson's Bay Company. Thompson, though, said nothing of how he felt about being sent to a strange world.

Plainly emboldened by Pareil's success, Côté asked, "How is it you are no longer with the Hudson's Bay Company?"

For a long moment Peter thought Thompson wouldn't answer, but finally he explained. "I was with them for more than six years and might still be had they not broken their promise to allow me to leave off trading for furs and survey and explore for them." Stretching out his leg, he knocked on it and went on. "I had broken this in a few places, and whilst it was mending, Mr. Turnor, their surveyor, taught me his craft as well as how to study the stars and soil and all things that grow. He loaned his books to me, as well. It was the most interesting winter of my life."

The group around the fire waited expectantly when Thompson paused and poked at the fire with a stick before he continued. "In all else the Hudson's Bay Company treated me well. After seven years, when my apprenticeship was finished, instead of the customary new suit of clothing, I asked for surveying instruments. They obliged me with a very good set as well as a ten-inch brass sextant and a salary of fifteen pounds a year. I used the money to buy more books."

"Why then ...?" Côté began, and was interrupted by Thompson.

"Why did I leave the company? It was as I said. I learned they had been given a mandate along with their large grant of land that obligated them to survey and explore for the good of England. That was why I signed on with them for another seven years. When it became known to me there would only be trading for furs and little surveying, I left with my good friend Boulard."

"It is true," Boulard said. "And what adventures we had in those first days when our good North West Company ordered you to survey the forty-ninth parallel and find the company posts that must be moved or discover themselves in the United States."

Vallade's eyes widened. "This is true?"

"Of course," Boulard retorted. "Did I not say as much? England and the Americans to the south agreed which land is theirs, and Monsieur Thompson made the line on the map that we may know also." He chuckled. "You may be certain there was much excitement when we learned that Grand Portage was six miles on the American side. They moved it pretty quick, I tell you."

Hoping Thompson would speak of these adventures, Peter started to ask a question of his own, but the mapmaker yawned and stretched, announcing it was time for bed.

As the days went by, and the hoped-for success in binding the boat boards together turned into failure, the builders became snappish. Dog, as though she sensed the mood of the camp, followed more closely on Peter's heels and leaped about to keep out of the way of the men. Finally, after a month of planning and working by trial and error, the boat was finished and ready to be tested in the river. Peter watched anxiously as it was lifted — two men on each end — to be taken to the water. Before they took three steps, however, it broke in half.

That night Peter heard Thompson confide in Boulard. "It's possible I ask too much of these men. I'm concerned that even men as loyal as these might become discouraged and leave us."

Boulard was silent for a moment before he replied. "They are accustomed to hardship, but hardship and work from dawn to dark without knowing if it will ever end is not good, my friend."

CHAPTER 13

By the time the canoe had been rebuilt and caulked with pitch stripped from the pine trees and heated, it was mid-April and the snow was fast disappearing along the river. The day the boat was launched was bright and clear, the air fragrant with wet cedar.

"A good omen," Thompson said after breakfast as he straightened from his crouch by the fire and squinted at the sun. He looked around. "I've named this place Boat Encampment with respect for our efforts here."

Boulard stood, hands on hips, surveying his surroundings. "It is certain never will I forget this place."

"Me, neither," Peter agreed, but for a different reason. He had grown fond of Boat Encampment. Here he had come to feel he was somebody — somebody with good memories of hardships and friendships with men who treated him as an equal.

The mapmaker studied each man in turn. "I wish to be certain that you understand my reasons not to follow the big river downstream and go to Kootenay House instead."

There was a murmur of assent from the men, and Vallade spoke up. "We are few, and our canoe may not be strong enough to carry us in places we have not been."

"And we will find men at Kootenay House and horses," Côté finished.

Reluctant as he was to say goodbye to their little home of cedar planks, Peter breathed a prayer that this time the canoe would hold together when Villiard and Pareil grasped the bow and Vallade and Côté lifted the other end, preparing to haul it to the water.

The canoe did stay together as it was lifted, and Peter cheered silently when it settled into the water like a big brown duck. Grasping the braided pine roots tied to the bow, he held it firmly close to the shore while the mounds of moose meat, tents, trade goods, and personal belongings were loaded. There had been some discussion as to whether there was room enough for Peter's too-long legs to allow him to kneel and paddle as did the rest of the men. At the end of the discussion the cargo was rearranged to make room. Peter then picked up a roughly hewn paddle and knelt at his place near the back of the canoe with Dog beside him and Boulard behind to instruct him in the art of paddling while he, himself, took care of the steering. Thompson stood in the bow with a pole to keep them from the rocks. The voyageurs began to sing.

In spite of the auspicious beginning, their canoe, clumsy and difficult to steer, carried them no more than twelve miles the first day. Still, they camped that night full of confidence that the following day would be better. But it wasn't.

They had spent the night huddled under the overturned canoe and awoke to find themselves beneath a foot of drifted snow. Nevertheless, the entire group remained cheerful, and forgoing breakfast, quickly had the craft righted and loaded again. That day it didn't snow, but a cold, wet fog engulfed them for slow, uncertain miles. A muffled voice spoke Peter's thoughts when it cried out in the mist, "Will nothing go well on this accursed journey!"

Their leader sounded tired as he responded with, "It will get better as we go south. However, I see there is more ice ahead. We best pull to shore."

They spent five miserable days hunched beside a fire of damp wood, waiting for the weather to clear and the ice jam to melt. Peter wondered if before they had started Thompson had suspected they would have so many troubles on the search for this river. He most likely wasn't all that happy with eating and sleeping day after day in the freezing cold, either, but he probably had the comfort of knowing someday that this would come to an end and he would have the satisfaction of knowing he hadn't faltered.

Peter had given some thought to what he would do after their journey ended. He might be hired as a clerk in a company post, but first he would have to get back over the mountains. He shuddered.

Although their journey continued thus for the first half of their trip to Kootenay House, few complained aloud. Compared to those miles, the second hundred were relatively easy. The weather warmed, and most of the ice and snow along the river disappeared. However, the back-breaking work of paddling and poling the heavy canoe upstream took its toll, and even Boulard questioned the need for hauling the heavy trade goods.

Thompson was firm but patient. "Until they find a

man to replace me, I'm responsible for the Columbia River District. And to make it profitable, I must find villages for trading. Also, as I told you at the beginning of our journey, we must have goods to offer as we go down the river. If we hurry by the Indian villages as we pass downstream with the current, will they not resent our intrusion into their territory without permission and view us as enemies? When we return slowly against the current, it may be too late to make friends with them."

That made sense to Peter, and to Boulard, as well, apparently. The voyageur nodded approval. "As always, you understand our Indian friends best. But, me, I am of the opinion we perhaps will arrive at the big ocean much later than the men sent by ship by Mr. Astor."

"Whether we do or not is of small importance," Thompson said. "My plan is to get the village people to promise to gather furs only for us. If they agree, there will be few furs for the American company no matter how many posts they build."

As they advanced up the river, the air seemed less cold, and on the willows they passed tiny green leaves were slowly unfurling. Peter's tired body gained new energy when Thompson announced they were nearing Kootenay House where they would find men to join them for the rest of the voyage.

However, Thompson was mistaken. Moments after he spoke they rounded a bend in the river and met a canoe of a half-dozen free traders. As one, the two canoes turned to the shore to exchange news.

Greetings were exchanged, and after Thompson related their purpose in ascending the river, one of the traders shook his head. "I'm told it's useless to go to this Kootenay House, for after some attention from the Peigans, it's empty."

"Do you have news of Finan McDonald, the man in charge of the post?" Thompson asked, his eyes anxious.

The trader and the men in his canoe shook their heads. "I'm sorry," the trader said. "Perhaps others have heard." He shrugged and picked up his paddle.

"A moment, please," Thompson said. Peering around the trader at a stocky Iroquois in the middle of the canoe, he called out, "Charles, is that you, my friend?"

The Indian grinned and nodded. "*Bonjour, monsieur.* I am Charles."

Thompson turned to the men in his own canoe. "Charles and I travelled these waters together many times when I was at Kootenay House. He's a very good man." Turning back, he said, "Charles, we'd consider it an honour if you'd accompany us on our voyage to the west. We have need of a good canoe man."

That was easy, Peter thought as the man clambered into their canoe. Long black hair blew freely beside his round face, and his grin revealed one front tooth was missing. In spite of the cool air blowing across the water, Charles wore no coat, and the rolled-up sleeves on his bright red shirt revealed bulging muscles on his arms. He took the pole from Thompson and stood in the bow of the boat.

When they reached Kootenay House, Peter was glad they had been warned that it had been deserted, for when they reached the landing below the stockade the ominous silence was broken only by the raucous cries of three crows circling overhead. Without speaking Boulard leaped from the canoe and climbed the path to the fort.

Almost reluctantly the rest followed in single file. It was clear that Kootenay House had been abandoned some time ago. A family of tree swallows had established residence close to the ceiling of the men's quarters. Peter followed Thompson as he moved from room to room in silence. When the search was completed, the mapmaker went outside to rejoin the men.

"There's no sign of a message from Finan McDonald," Thompson said. "We best go on to Salish House in the morning. He may have moved the trade goods there."

Peter thought it felt good to spread his bedroll in a room with a solid roof, though there was something eerie about this empty post. Sighing deeply, he turned on his side and threw his arm over Dog, who was stretched out beside him. When he was warned by a low growl, he sighed again.

In the morning, to save on their dried meat, breakfast had to wait until Boulard and Pareil returned from a barely successful hunting effort. They carried a thin carcass of a mule deer between them. In response to the half-joking complaints from the rest of the men, Boulard blamed the late winter for the lack of fat on their contribution to breakfast. Although the meat was undeniably tough, it was quickly consumed and the canoe was packed.

Boulard had said that he had lived at this post for three years with Thompson and his family, and they had created trading posts along the river. Wondering how long their next journey would be, Peter asked, "How far away is Salish House?"

"Not far," Thompson said. "Downstream we have to drag our canoe across a strip of land to a river nearby that will take us down to the Salish Indian Road. We'll leave the canoe there and walk through some very fine country until we reach Clark's Fork. I'm certain we'll find both hunters and traders there."

Thompson was right about the country, Peter thought. With Dog at his heels he trotted through the warm grass of a meadow dotted with patches of early spring flowers, mixtures of white and yellow. Behind were blue mountains topped with snow that sparkled in the sunlight, and ahead was a forest of deep green conifers sharing space with newly leafed aspen and birch. For the first time in months Peter was warm deep into his bones. He tried to lengthen his steps to keep up with the man striding along beside him whose name was Ignace.

The newcomer had been with a hunting party they had met when they stopped to rest on Tobacco Plains. Knowing that Ignace was another excellent canoe man, Thompson had hired him for their voyage down the Columbia River. When they reached Salish Indian Road, Ignace had been very helpful in finding a safe place to stow their canoe and the trade goods, greatly lessening the burden for each man to carry. Nevertheless, Peter was looking forward to the horses Thompson had promised to get when they reached Salish House. He felt safer on a horse somehow. Knowing this Salish Indian Road was on Native war grounds, each of the party had readied his gun and walked with it now at waist level.

Peter was gratified to see Ignace was barely taller than himself, and when the man glanced over at him and grinned, Peter wished he could speak Iroquois. Perhaps he could try sign language, though he wasn't certain how to go about it. The only time he had seen sign language used was in the trade room at Rocky Mountain House, and he wasn't sure what the gestures had meant. Thinking hard, Peter didn't notice the men ahead of him had stopped suddenly. He recoiled as his foot collided with Boulard's boot and his gun jammed the voyageur in the back.

Before Peter could apologize Boulard turned and put a hand over Peter's mouth. "Ahead, there in the woods, someone speaks," he whispered.

The rest of the men had dropped to their knees, guns ready. Peter and Boulard followed suit and waited in the tall grass. Hearing a rumble in Dog's chest, Peter grasped her collar and warned her not to make a sound. Then, peering over Boulard's shoulder, he stared at the grove of trees less than a hundred feet away.

Chapter 14

The bushes parted slowly and out stepped two young women dressed in buckskin trousers and tunics beaded with intricate designs around the necks and sleeves. When they caught sight of the men, they immediately halted and their eyes dropped to the muskets pointed at them. They stood helplessly awaiting their fate.

When Thompson called out to them, the girls looked up, their faces filled with delight. Running closer, they chattered as they did so, and Peter was certain he heard one speak the explorer's name. Boulard verified this by whispering, "They remember David when he traded in their village. They are Salish."

Thompson turned and repeated Boulard's comment. "They're Salish. They'll lead us to their camp."

The camp was a village of about forty tents and home to the chief of all the Salish. He, as well as the rest of his people, was plainly pleased to have Thompson and his companions as guests. Soon the entire group was seated in a wide circle around a fire with the chief and elders of the tribe. Food seemed to come from everywhere, and after the steady diet of deer and moose meat, the plentiful meal of steelhead trout and camas root was very welcome. Peter's wooden bowl was refilled twice before he put it down. Beside him Côté poked him with an elbow. Nodding in the direction of Thompson and the chief, he said, "Our mapmaker does not eat — only talk, talk, talk. He frowns many times, and you will notice the chief does not look so happy, as well. Perhaps we are not so welcome as we thought."

Clearly, Boulard had overheard, for he leaned forward to peer around the hatchet-faced young warrior beside him and said, "I have travelled here with Monsieur Thompson before and also understand the language of these people. We are welcome. The chief is not happy and Monsieur Thompson frowns because the Peigans have been raiding villages on this side of the mountains. Because of the Peigans, Monsieur Finan McDonald was forced to leave Kootenay House."

Peter grew increasingly uneasy. In order not to run into the Peigans, they had struggled along the Athabasca and again upstream on what Thompson now thought was the Columbia. But after all that would they be troubled by the Peigans now? He waited impatiently for the food to be taken away and the pipe to be passed around the circle so he could learn more from Thompson, but the pipe kept moving from man to man and the talking didn't stop.

A thin sliver of moon was high above the trees by the time Peter heard the mapmaker's footsteps approaching. The brigade had walked far that day, and Peter had finally given in to the fatigue that had plagued him ever since his stomach had been filled. After he put up the tent he shared with Boulard, he had dropped onto his blankets with Dog at his feet, but Boulard had waited outside. Waking from a nap, Peter heard the two men talking.

"We won't find Finan McDonald at Salish House, either," Thompson said. "He's been threatened by the Peigans there, as well. One of the free traders told the Salish that Finan has moved his trade goods to the post on Little Spokane River.

"This is the one you sent Jaco Finlay to build three years past, is it not?" Boulard asked.

Thompson must have nodded, for Peter heard, "Let's hope if this isn't true that Finan left some word at Salish House before he abandoned it. It will soon be impossible to supply posts that move about willy-nilly."

"Let us also hope they did not burn Salish House," Boulard said.

"That they wouldn't do," Thompson said. "Though not for any consideration of the North West Company. The Peigans have too much respect for trees and animals and wouldn't risk a forest fire."

Peter heard no more, for he had slipped into a sound sleep.

In the morning, with some skilful bargaining, the mapmaker obtained a horse for each of them and promptly sent Ignace, Côté, and Pareil back to collect the trade goods they had cached. "We meet at Salish House," he said before they cantered away. "While there we'll build a canoe so that we can deposit most of our trade goods at Kullyspell House."

Before the sun achieved its zenith, they reached the Clark's Fork River and the deserted Salish House. Certain this time there had to be a message from Finan McDonald, they searched both the inside and the outside of the cabins twice but to no avail. Thompson made no comment, but Peter sensed his frustration when he abruptly ordered Vallade and Charles to hunt for game and the rest to look for white cedar to build a canoe.

The men sang as they set to work constructing the canoe, but Thompson appeared worried. "The river's rising two feet a day," he cautioned. "Our boat must be sturdy and the paddles strong." He grew even more concerned when a little more than a week later the boat was ready and their hunters had found only small game to keep everyone fed as they worked, but none for their journey. After Ignace, Côté, and Pareil returned with the cache of trade goods, the Salish braves who had accompanied them gathered up the borrowed horses and prepared to leave. Thompson stopped them to bargain with tobacco and powder, and the Salish agreed the voyageurs could have a plump filly to slaughter for meat to take in the canoe as they shot down the Clark's Fork River.

Much later, after they took their places in the canoe, Peter wasn't surprised when Thompson ordered him to sit in the back. They now had enough men to paddle, and experience would be needed to navigate the rapids ahead. "May God guide us," Thompson said. He then hopped into the canoe and sat beside Peter. Dog crouched between boxes of trade goods, and Boulard enthroned himself on a sack of flour.

Charles gave the bobbing vessel a mighty shove into the fast-moving water before leaping in to take his place at the bow. Accustomed though he was now to travelling on water, Peter felt his heart hammer as they flew with the current — Boulard determinedly keeping the canoe in the middle of the river.

In spite of Boulard's efforts the current often tossed the boat in front of the small islands he tried to avoid, and sometimes they found themselves tipping downward through a series of eddies or twirling in a whirlpool. Each night the battered canoe had to be turned over to dry, and in the morning it had to be freshly caulked with heated pitch scraped from the pines found in the woods along the way. Also each night Thompson led the men in a prayer of thanks for keeping them safe that day and another to ask for an equally safe journey the next day.

"We must cross the lake that two years earlier I named Pend Oreille to reach the Pend Oreille River," Thompson said in the morning. "Praise God it should be less furious than this one. With good fortune we should reach Kullyspell where we'll give the trading goods to James McMillan and build a better canoe to proceed down to the mouth of the Columbia."

Peter admired the mapmaker's ability to recall each river individually, for he was right about the Pend Oreille. In some places it was over its banks, but it had no islands or rocks midstream and the current was swift but not treacherous. Peter relaxed and, no longer fearing Dog might get frightened and leap from the canoe, he let go of the braided rope around her neck.

Before the end of the day they reached Kullyspell House and found that McMillan had already left for his annual trip east over the mountains. Except for twelve tents of Kullyspell Indians camped beside the lake, this post, too, was deserted. Luckily, Thompson understood enough of the language of the people camping there to converse with them for several minutes. When he returned to the men in the canoe, he said, "I'm told our elusive Finan McDonald is with Jaco Finlay at Spokane House, thus I've hired two of the men here to find him and tell him to bring horses to carry our goods."

That was good news to Peter, and judging by the grins of relief on the faces of the tired voyageurs, it made them happy, too. The Kullyspell people were very friendly and insisted on preparing a feast for them. That night they dined on baked fish, dog, some sort of waterfowl, and bread that Thompson said was made of moss hanging from trees. Peter found it dry and hard to swallow, and Dog refused it totally.

Peter didn't hear all that Thompson had to say to Finan McDonald when the company man finally arrived with three men and thirteen extra horses, but it must have been serious. As they parted that night, Thompson called after McDonald, "Try to remember that the Peigans aren't bad people and that most of them are our friends."

McDonald didn't reply. Nor did he even turn around when Thompson spoke. The next day, however, when they began the two-day trip to Spokane House, Peter was relieved to see that the tension between the two men had disappeared and they were able to discuss amiably the problems of transporting trade goods over the mountains.

"A good road can be made through the pass where the Athabasca begins," Thompson insisted, "provided it's travelled only in summer months."

McDonald had doubts. "When the Peigans learn of it, they'll block that, as well."

"I disagree. That far north they risk a confrontation with the Cree as well as with the traders who will be well armed to defend themselves."

"I haven't been to the mountains so far north," McDonald admitted. "What about horses?"

Thompson shook his head. "Horses wouldn't be useful until the headwaters are reached and it's too shallow for canoes. A post could be made there to keep packhorses for the distance to the great river at a place I call Boat Encampment." McDonald looked at Thompson, a question in his eyes, and the mapmaker said, "Yes, the great Columbia River. I'm almost certain now that I've found its source up in the mountains."

"Then why —" McDonald began.

Knowing what the question would be, Thompson interrupted to give McDonald the same reasons he had given to his men as to why they first went to Kootenay House rather than risk their canoe on what he thought was the Columbia River. The mapmaker finished by saying, "Still, I can't be certain we were at its source until we reach the great ocean and return upstream."

Peter shivered again when he thought of the return across the mountains. Thompson had said it would be before winter, and he hoped he was right. But it was now mid-June and they still hadn't reached the big ocean or even knew how far away it was. He sighed inwardly as he remembered how good it had been to sleep in the cabin at Whitemud House. He had awakened there to the smell of porridge. And there would be real bread and carrots and onions. Peter felt his mouth watering.

Two days after they arrived at Spokane House they prepared for the ride north to a place called Kettle Falls where David hoped to find both guides and information on the people as well as on the river they would travel.

It took four days of steady riding to reach the place, making it necessary at times for Peter to stop and boost a weary Dog up to share his saddle.

Côté laughed when he first saw Dog draped in front of Peter. "Is it not strange your friend will allow you to take her up to give her rest but refuses the caress on the head?"

"Maybe she has a headache," Peter said shortly. It was a sore point that Dog still growled and backed away if he tried to pet her. Then, reminding himself it wasn't Côté's fault, he hastened to add, "Maybe she still has pain."

Côté nodded and clicked his tongue sympathetically. "From Monsieur DuNord."

Peter had forgotten about DuNord, and he wondered now if the man and his companions had made it back to Rocky Mountain House. He wondered, too, what they would have to say about Thompson's expedition when they got there. Just then the sounds of axes on wood accompanying the shouts of children and barking dogs cut into his thoughts. Ahead was Kettle Falls and the largest village of tents Peter had yet seen on this trip.

Recalling an earlier description he had heard of a gathering of the tribes for war, Peter thought this was what he was seeing, but he quickly dismissed that idea when he noticed the children chasing one another and the women gossiping and laughing as they scrubbed clothing on the rocks along a backwater above the falls.

Thompson put up a hand to halt his small train of men and horses, obviously pleased. "This is much better than I expected. Kettle Falls is a common rendezvous for several tribes to trade and exchange news, but I dared not hope we'd find so many here. There are sure to be more than one who will tell us where we'll encounter dangerous rapids as well as the best places to stop and hunt for game."

The explorer raised his hand in greeting as two solemn Indian men approached. When they drew close, Thompson swung off his horse and moved to meet them. Peter didn't strain to hear their conversation. He knew he wouldn't understand the language. Instead he looked back at the children who had gathered nearby and seemed to be staring at him. He glanced down at Dog still draped in the saddle in front of him. "I guess they've never seen a dog ride a horse before."

The children hooted with laughter as though they had understood his words. Dog gave a short bark, and the children laughed again.

Beside Peter, Vallade commented, "And never perhaps did they hear an animal in conversation with her master."

The children laughed even harder.

Thompson had finished speaking with the elder, and with a wave at the children, Peter turned his horse to follow the mapmaker to the end of a half-circle of tents. "We'll camp here," Thompson said, "until we get a proper canoe built — one that will withstand rough waters." To Peter's surprise, Thompson turned to him and said, "See that your dog is kept from the village beasts lest they attack. We may have need of her."

Chapter 15

There were no birch trees to be found on the windswept hills, and locating good cedar to cut into lengths for their boat was far more difficult than Thompson had thought it would be. They were forced to cut boards from many different trees, and most had to be carried more than five miles to the riverbank. Working from sun-up to sundown, however, the crew managed to finish the canoe in four days. So, early one morning near the beginning of July, they left by first light for the final journey down the Columbia.

Clearly, the men enjoyed the challenge as they guided the craft through foaming cascades, laughing and shouting as they fought to keep it in the middle of the river. Peter grasped the rope on Dog's collar tightly and watched the scenery sweep past. It was a warm, sunny day, and in the meadows long grass mixed with purple, white, and blue flowers swayed in the steady breeze. Occasionally, he saw stands of trees smaller than those along the Kootenay and not so close together.

"Fifty-six miles," Thompson called from the bow of the canoe, pointing to a wide stream pouring into the Columbia. "Spokane River," he added.

In the late afternoon they landed not far from a small village made of poles covered with rushes. It was home to the Indians Thompson had hired at Kettle Falls. Before the men leaped from the canoe they tossed their paddles into the grass growing along the shore. Peter had seen them do this before and had wondered why. This time, pointing to a long black snake that shot from the grass and slithered quickly down a path, Thompson turned to Peter. "You see now why we may have need of your dog. That one is very dangerous, and your dog would find it before we did."

A thrill of fear for his pet rippled up Peter's spine. He grasped the rope he had fastened to Dog tightly and pulled the protesting animal to a tree close to where they were to wait for the village elders.

The Simpoil leaders arrived one by one, and when they were all seated, the chief, a dignified, wrinkled man with stone-grey hair tied in two braids, presented Thompson with a basket of roots and onions and two large salmon. Peter was delighted. Salmon was a fish he liked, and these were large enough for all of them to have a feast. His mouth watered and his stomach rumbled again. Beside him Boulard poked him in the ribs and whispered, "Order the voice inside to be quiet, *s'il vous plaît*, so that I may hear these important words."

Peter grinned at his friend ruefully. He knew the smoking of the pipe would take time. With close attention he watched as the long, elegantly carved pipe was filled and offered to the sun and the wind in all four directions. The chief smoked first and then passed the pipe to Thompson who, after his turn, handed it to the elder next to him. When the pipe completed the circle, the conversation began.

Although the sun had long since dipped behind them, there seemed to be no indication that the chief would stop talking so his guests could eat. Bored with listening to words he didn't understand, Peter amused himself by staring at the chief and willing him to stop talking. To his astonishment the chief sat down abruptly. However, it took almost as long for the interpreter to repeat the words — thanks for the arrival of the white man and hope that the next time Thompson came to the village he would bring guns, powder, axes, knives, steel, flints, and many other items. The chief's interpreter said the Simpoil would pay for all that was brought to them. Right now they had only their hands and weak arrows to get game.

Thompson seemed to listen to the chief's words with great care and promised to bring all he requested and more provided he gave them accurate information on the big river, particularly how well large, heavily laden canoes could travel up it.

Later, as at last they sat in a wide circle and dined on the salmon, deer meat, and berries the women had prepared, Peter found he was seated next to a young Simpoil barely older than himself. On the other side was one of the interpreters. With the interpreter's help the Simpoil youth asked, "You find the meat to your liking?"

Peter nodded. "If your weapons aren't good, how do you kill deer?"

"Many hunt in a big circle," the young man explained. "With care we move to make the circle smaller and smaller until we are close enough to kill the deer we find." He stared at the fire sadly. "Arrows of flint often do not kill, and the deer run away."

Peter felt guilty that he was eating something that had been so difficult to obtain, so he decided not to take a fourth piece.

Thompson was so intent on getting as much information about the Columbia as possible that they didn't leave until noon the next day. By early afternoon, they found another village where they had to stop and smoke with the people. Plainly, the Indians were unafraid of the white strangers and listened intently as the mapmaker described his reasons for coming to their village. They nodded at one another happily and then at Thompson when the interpreters translated his message. As Thompson talked, some of the villagers walked around Peter and the rest of the voyageurs, peering at their clothing and hair. Later, when Côté and Vallade used axes to split driftwood for their fire, their efforts were regarded with wonder.

Watching the village people, Peter thought of the times he had found life hard. Sometimes he had known hunger in Montreal, and many times they had had little to eat while crossing the mountains and beyond. But knowing the hunger would end when they returned east had made it easier to bear. Here the people had little to look forward to but search for food, make rush mats to cover the poles for their house, and find driftwood to burn. They didn't seem unhappy, but he didn't envy them, and he hoped the company would bring goods to make life easier for them. When they waved goodbye the next morning, he felt depressed.

At times, when the current appeared to slow, the men

lifted their oars and allowed the canoe to drift down the river. The terrain on both sides of the river seemed to be drier and less fertile now. The soil was greyish-white, and the grass grew in short clumps. The pungent scent of sagebrush filled their nostrils when the breeze blew over the river, and the cries of hawks sounded eerily in the silence as they spiralled overhead.

Indian camps appeared more frequently now, and each time they did Thompson ordered the men to pull for shore. With the aid of the Simpoil interpreters, he engaged the Indians in conversation, always explaining he was there to learn if it was possible to bring trade goods down the river. Without fail both men and women seemed more than happy to agree to trap for furs and trade them for the goods Thompson would bring.

It was easy to see now that some of the voyageurs were getting impatient with the time spent at these villages — stops that lasted anywhere from an hour to all night. But Thompson wouldn't risk offending any of the Indians along the way. "They're good people," he said. "They ask for very little."

By Thompson's calculations they were at a village near the confluence of the Snake River when the Simpoil said it would be useless to go farther since they didn't know the languages of the people down the river. "This is trouble," Boulard said.

Thompson appeared unconcerned, though. "There are a man and his wife here who wish to return with us to their village downriver."

Boulard seemed surprised. "They speak our language?"

Thompson shook his head. "Charles, our steersman,

speaks a little of the man's tongue. He's the one who told me the man wishes to go with us. I think he'll prove to be of help."

Charles was able to translate, but in Peter's opinion this made conversations with village people even more lengthy and tedious. Thompson, however, was pleased, for several of the chiefs they met asked for a post to be built on the river, and he promised that would be done where the Snake River emptied into the Columbia.

Peter received that bit of information with dismay. Did that mean they would have to camp long enough to build a fort? he wondered. With each day that passed it had become increasingly clear that when they returned to the east they again would cross the height of land in the winter. It was an effort to keep his feelings from showing on his face when they reached the waters of the Snake and Thompson ordered the boat to shore. But Peter breathed a sigh of relief when the mapmaker announced they wouldn't camp there. On Thompson's orders Côté and Vallade stripped a tall pine of most of its branches, then the explorer firmly tied a paper to the tree.

While Thompson stared up at the paper, lost in thought, the men whispered, "What is it on the paper? What does he say?"

Peter read the notice carefully, then said, "The paper is a claim to the land all around this place in the name of England. And it states that the North West Company will build a trading post here." He examined the paper again. "And Mr. Thompson signed his name and the date — 8 July 1811."

If their leader had planned a small ceremony to

honour the occasion, he must have been disappointed, for the men granted him only a quick cheer and leaped back into the boat, ready to take on the mighty river again.

The Columbia widened to about eight hundred yards as it carried them southwest on fairly placid water. Suddenly, on the left, a huge white mountain loomed over the trees. It was so perfectly shaped in a cone that Peter thought it looked as though it had been drawn on a piece of blue paper. From his place in the bow Thompson said, "That mountain is called Hood. It was first seen by the captain of a ship named the *Columbia*, hence the name of this river."

Silently, Peter rejoiced. Months ago Thompson had spoken of Mount Hood. This had to mean they were near their destination. If there were no more rapids, perhaps they would be at the mouth of the river in a few days. However, the calm of the Columbia proved to be deceptive when Thompson suddenly called out a warning to Charles.

The mapmaker pointed at the walls of rock that jutted menacingly into the river, shrinking its width to less than a hundred feet. Even from that distance Peter could see the river raging high against the vertical slabs of basalt that forced the water into a boiling torrent. As one man, the paddlers pulled hard for the shore, but they made little headway as their canoe gained speed and the current swept it sideways toward the rocks.

The velocity of the current kept increasing, and Peter anxiously watched the efforts of the men as they paddled more rapidly than ever before. One moment they seemed to gain distance, and in another instant they appeared to be losing their struggle until Boulard, waving his arms and shouting, urged Charles to point the helpless craft at an angle to the shore. When the steersman did so, it seemed they were getting closer to the beach, but the cliffs loomed close enough now to cast a shadow on the small boat.

About ten feet out Charles suddenly leaped into water up to his chest, the rope in his hand, and began to pull. Boulard, too, jumped in, followed by Vallade, and waded to the bow of the canoe to help the steersman. Following Thompson's lead, Peter snatched one of the paddles they had dropped. His arms ached with his efforts to help keep the back of the canoe from swinging around and allow the current to broadside the canoe, and his breath came in ragged gasps. Long moments passed before the boat landed on a narrow strip of stones and dirt not more than fifty feet from the first perpendicular slab of rock.

No one spoke until the canoe had been pulled out of the water and they had dropped beside it. It was Charles who broke the silence when he glared at the two passengers they carried and shouted at them angrily. The woman seemed frightened, but the man rose from his seat on the ground and answered in kind. The conversation lasted for several minutes before Charles turned to Thompson, disgust written on his face. "He say people of the village where we stopped did not tell him bad waters were ahead. He say we passed his village. They go back now."

Boulard's eyes followed the man and his wife as they walked upstream along the river. Dripping water, the big voyageur trotted after them when they disappeared around a sharp bend about a half-mile away. Peter, meanwhile, sat with the rest of the group staring upward at the sheer face of the hill they had to climb. It appeared to be impossible. For a moment even the mapmaker looked defeated, but his face changed quickly when Boulard reappeared, calling his name. "David, there is a way. The man and his woman followed a trail made by animals."

"A trail for animals, not men, to be sure," Côté grumbled as they struggled up the zigzag path, sometimes pulling, sometimes carrying the canoe.

Boulard heard and replied with in an exaggerated tone of hurt, "Me, I am very happy I have the great intelligence to find this trail. Perhaps you would prefer to fly in the canoe over the water?"

As the two men bantered back and forth, Peter's feelings of admiration came to the fore again. When Thompson agreed they would portage on that trail, Boulard had been the first to jump hip-deep into the river to push the heavy canoe along the shore while Côté had snatched the bow rope to pull. They had managed to get their craft upstream again to the beginning of the trail where each, including Peter, made two trips uphill and downhill until they crossed the land above the rocks, carrying bales and boxes of goods and the hindquarter of a horse, the last of their food.

The work was heavy, but no one stopped to rest. The man and woman who had disappeared might be blameless, but then again they could have hurried to tell their village of the big canoe and what it carried. If the village was large, the brigade could be hopelessly outnumbered.

CHAPTER 16

The mapmaker had no way of communicating with the few Indians they saw in the next two days, but from their gestures he thought there might be some falls and carrying places ahead. He was right, much to Peter's relief, for it was beyond tiring to sit all day in the canoe and brush mosquitoes away from his face and off Dog's nose. Surprisingly, she didn't snap or growl when he did so, leaving Peter to believe the tiny bugs bothered her plenty, too.

Their canoe reached a series of low cascades studded by huge rocks that didn't discourage the voyageurs at all. *"Allez!"* Charles shouted, and the canoe shot over the first drop to dip its bow into the white foam and back up again, darting and weaving between the rocks. Clutching Dog's rope and drenched with spray, Peter laughed. He envied Charles and vowed that someday he, too, would steer through rapids.

More rapids appeared, but this time Thompson was watching for them. In spite of his men's entreaties, the mapmaker ordered the voyageurs to pull for shore.

"Regard the small distance through which we must

go," Boulard coaxed. "It is better for these men than unloading, carrying, and loading again."

With the cries of agreement from the rest of the paddlers, Thompson finally consented. "First, however, I'll remove my instruments and goods." He nodded to Peter. "I'm not an oarsman, nor are you. Get your goods and come ashore." As an afterthought, he added, "And be sure not to leave behind the drawings you've made for me."

Peter, too, had been doubtful about running the rapids ahead. Not only were there rocks, but a large island in the middle of the river narrowed it into two channels, each with huge trees leaning almost horizontally to the middle of the water.

It was one of the trees, not a rock, that caused the trouble.

With Dog at his heels Peter trailed after Thompson downstream, planting each foot carefully on the slippery rocks and crawling around the trees overhanging both water and shore. The men in the boat had to rearrange the cargo to redistribute the weight, thus Peter and Thompson had almost reached the shore at the end of the rapids where calm water flowed before the men pushed back into midstream. The rushing water was too noisy for Peter to hear the cries of the men until they were almost opposite him, but he saw that they seemed to be trying to turn the canoe. At the same moment Thompson dropped his box of instruments and pulled off his boots. Seconds later he was in the water, hanging on to the branches of a huge cedar stretched across the surface.

Peter stood transfixed, watching as the mapmaker

released his grip on the tree and flung himself farther into the river, only to whirl helplessly in the cascade until his arms again struck the cedar. Thompson grasped a leafless branch and clung to it as what appeared to be a bundle of clothes floated almost out of his reach. The explorer lunged into the current once more and grabbed the coat on the body bobbing toward him, giving it a mighty tug and hauling it back to the tree. Shocked, Peter saw that the bundle was Pareil. Gasping and coughing, the two men worked their way along the trunk of the tree until they reached the shore. The canoe landed downstream a few yards, and Boulard raced up to help the two men to a warm spot on a large boulder.

While Boulard and the paddlers aided the two drenched men in stripping off their clothes, Peter left the rocks with Dog to search for twigs. He returned with a small pile to start a fire under a fat log of driftwood. "Good lad," Thompson gasped as he struggled for breath. "We'll camp here tonight, and by morning our trousers should be dry."

Peter retreated to sit away from the men and savour the mapmaker's unexpected praise. He felt uncommonly lighthearted, so much so that he had to put a hand over his mouth to hide his grin when he saw the stocky Thompson climb a hill in his long underwear and look west through his telescope.

Returning to the fire, Thompson stood with his hands outstretched to warm them and spoke the words Peter had been waiting for ever since they had started down the river. "I believe I can see Point Vancouver," he said plainly, trying to conceal his excitement. "More than once I've read Captain Vancouver's account of surveying the river this far. Tomorrow we may see the Pacific Ocean."

Thompson was mistaken by one day. It took two days to reach Tongue Point and a view of the Pacific. The explorer seemed astonished when all the men voiced their disappointment.

"Me, I see Lake Winnipeg with waves much larger," Vallade declared, and the rest agreed.

"Think of it, men," Thompson said. "The country of Japan is opposite where we stand. It's five thousand miles across that water."

"For this we have come so far?" Pareil lamented. "I am sad."

Thompson scowled and was about to speak when he observed the twinkle in Pareil's eyes. "Wait until we reach the very end of this river," he told the voyageur. "Your thoughts will change."

They returned to the canoe, and after paddling about two miles, they spotted a cluster of four low cabins. On a short pole fluttered the American flag, with another banner below it displaying lettering they couldn't read. Without expression Thompson said, "I believe that to be John Jacob Astor's fur-trading post."

Peter looked up quickly to see if Thompson was disappointed that the Americans had beaten them to the ocean, but his features showed nothing.

There were no tents, but a half-dozen men who appeared to be Indians were hauling wood, and two men emerged from one of the buildings to welcome their visitors. Peter started in surprise. He recognized the men — Duncan McDougall and David Stuart. They had been working in the office of the North West Company when he left Montreal with Boulard, and now they seemed to be employed by the Pacific Fur Company.

If Thompson bore any resentment for these men deserting his own company in favour of Astor's, he kept it to himself. Instead he smiled warmly. "It's a pleasure for me and my companions to be here at last and to present you with this letter."

It wasn't sealed, and Thompson gestured for McDougall to read it. When the man finished reading, he handed the letter to Stuart, who whistled sharply as he folded the papers and returned them to Thompson.

"'Tis a surprise, for certain," McDougall said. "We haven't been told the North West Company was planning to buy a partnership in our company. Does this mean then you'll be expecting to use our trade room and the like?"

Thompson chuckled. "Not at all, my friend. And it's my understanding our company didn't wish to purchase a full partnership. Only a share."

Both of Astor's men were visibly relieved, and Peter knew why. As a full partner in the North West Company, David Thompson would have reduced the presence here of McDougall and Stuart back to the status of clerks. In addition the four small cabins were undoubtedly already crowded.

"Come then," Stuart said, beckoning to the rest of Thompson's men. "It's near time for supper. Let us share some of our bounty from the ocean with you. I guarantee you'll enjoy it."

This friendly atmosphere lasted for the few days the Canadian voyageurs rested at Fort Astoria, though the conversation became guarded when the subject turned to building forts and trading with the Indians. Peter was grateful that McDougall and Stuart made certain the Native woman who cooked for them served plenty of food — the best they had to offer. There was fresh salmon, deer, and things in shells from the sea. He decided he liked the last.

After they felt rested, Thompson gathered his men and announced they were going seven miles west to Cape Disappointment — the very end of the river. It was there that the men first accepted the immensity of the ocean as they watched each wave begin far out on the horizon and grow higher and higher as it rushed onward to hurl itself far up onto the shore.

Contemplating the wild collision between the river and the ocean, Thompson said, "I was told that only a few months earlier a ship called the *Tonquin* lost eight of its crew when they tried to row over that."

Peter noticed Côté cross himself and was certain the man was praying they wouldn't be expected to row in that place.

While they stared at the sea, Thompson said to no one in particular, "We've wet our feet in the great Pacific, but we must find our way back up this river to finish the task we set out to do."

Chapter 17

Thompson wanted to leave immediately after he saw the Pacific, for one of the men at Fort Astoria had reported they had been plagued with ague and fevers since they had arrived there. The mapmaker didn't want any of his own men to become afflicted. Still, he was curious about the three loaded dugouts tied at the fort and decided to wait another day or two to see what was to be done with them.

"I was told the dugouts were to meet Monsieur Astor's overland traders who are to arrive very soon," Boulard said.

Thompson's smile was grim. "I was told the same, but I think it's more likely they plan to build a post inland and wish to keep it secret from us. If we travel upriver together, we may discover where it will be."

Boulard shrugged. "Perhaps that is not so much a concern. Even Monsieur McDougall agrees that much of his goods are of little use and are poorly made. They are not what the Indians wish to receive in trade for their furs."

Glumly, Peter took his place in the canoe beside Dog for the return trip up the river. There was barely more than one week left in July and still the mountains to cross after they reached the headwaters of the river — if this was the Columbia. Thompson wasn't absolutely certain he was right. To make matters worse, the explorer had given the Astor men the impression that many of the Indians along the river were hostile, and it would be best for all the boats to travel together.

Even Boulard grumbled about that. "When we must portage, it is enough to carry that which we must have for ourselves, but now we must add the strange dugouts of this place?"

Charles agreed. "Dugout — she is nothing for men of the river. It is useless to put sail to her when wind good."

When the muttering reached Thompson's ears, he called the men together. "In exchange for travelling with them, Astor's men have promised us a few goods to trade for food as we proceed up the river. It will save us time we would otherwise need for hunting. As for carrying their goods, they have trade goods to pay those in the villages for carrying their dugouts."

After three days of hard paddling and sometimes pulling the boats from the shore, a party of Indians was seen seining for salmon, and, as one, the steersmen directed their vessels to the bank. The brigade was out of meat and nightfall was fast closing in on them.

When Thompson and Stuart got out of their boats and called out greetings, they were surprised and discomfited to find themselves ignored. Stuart beckoned to one of his men who knew the language of the fishermen. Although the man tried for several minutes to interest the Indians in trading goods for salmon, he received only surly glances in return. Thompson reached into his canoe and brought out a double handful of blue beads that he knew were favourites among the Columbian Natives. When he offered them to the two men, they stared back at him for a moment, hatred in their eyes, then pulled in their nets and stalked away.

As he waited in the canoe, Peter saw Côté swiftly make the sign of the cross and heard him murmur, "I think I do not care for this."

Anxiously wishing Thompson and Stuart would get back into their boats before the Indians returned with more men, Peter paid little attention to their discussion.

"Nevertheless I fail to understand this," Thompson said. "These people were friendly enough when we passed by them a few days earlier."

Stuart regarded the mapmaker with suspicion. "And I again ask if you're certain you know nothing you or your men did to persuade them to be hostile?"

Thompson drew himself up, suddenly every inch the man in charge of the Columbia District for the North West Company, and scowled at the Fort Astoria trader. "Sir," he said sternly, "I believe I, too, could ask that question. As for myself, I can truthfully state nothing untoward happened when we met with these people."

Stuart's face turned almost as red as his hair, and he shook his head. "Those two Indians haven't been seen at our post, thus I know of no reason for their hostility."

"There it is then," the mapmaker said. "It may be best we take our leave."

A half-mile up the river the water rushed around a series of huge rocks poking out of the riverbed, but the men insisted it would be easy to weave through them. As they laboured, a canoe carrying six Indians caught up with them. The one in the bow signalled for them to pull ashore. Peter was glad they did, for the Natives were offering four large salmon. Whatever they were given in return, they seemed very happy. A fire was built on the spot, and the salmon was cooked on the rocks in the centre of it.

When the meal was finished, one of the Indians stood and spoke while the Fort Astoria man translated. "When you came down this river, we found life good. But now we learn white men will bring sickness to us and giants to overturn our villages. We have given you food. Are we all to die?"

Thompson told the interpreter to say, "I speak the truth. No one has brought a sickness, and there are no giants to overturn your villages. And I remind you that only the Great Spirit has that power." When he finished, the Indians appeared satisfied.

The portage around the huge slabs of basalt that had narrowed the river on the way down wasn't so difficult this time. The bluff on this side of the river was only half as high, and the path was much wider. The canoe could be carried, but the dugouts could only be dragged with the help of the men of the North West Company.

As they proceeded in the following days, the rapids they had shot so gleefully on the journey down to the ocean were more and more difficult as they paddled and poled against the current, frequently making it necessary to carry the canoe. The Fort Astoria dugouts, however, sometimes proved to be impossible to hoist up the banks and over the rocks, forcing Stuart to hire Indians who seemed to appear from nowhere. For the most part they were tribe members Thompson hadn't spoken with before. At one series of rapids the Natives were inclined to be troublesome.

It took some time, but when Stuart finally came to a trade agreement with the young Indians he hired to help his men carry the boats, Boulard was scandalized with the price that was paid and with the behaviour of the Natives. Halfway through their job, they demanded payment, and Stuart was forced to agree, even though he wasn't sure which of the crowd of men had helped. As he tried to puzzle that out, the Indians pulled out their double daggers and began to sharpen them with a stone dipped in the water. Understanding their message, Stuart opened a box of trade goods and doled out at least five times the agreed price to every man there.

Thompson, who had calmly watched this transaction take place, beckoned to Stuart after the last of his tobacco had been given out. "Stand here beside me," he told the Fort Astoria man softly. Peter noted that the long-barrelled pistols Thompson usually left in the boat were hanging by his side. "They're spoiling for a fight. It would be an excuse to take all we have."

Peter gulped and began to back slowly up the slope toward Boulard and the rest of the men beside the canoe. As he drew closer, he could see the muskets they hid behind them, and he reached into the canoe for his own.

The Indians began to dance. Closer and closer, a dozen or more pranced about waving their daggers until one, bolder than the rest, swept his close to Thompson's chest. Almost casually, the mapmaker swung up his pistol and drew an arc on the other man's buckskin shirt, causing him to back away so quickly he fell over a rock. At almost that same instant a voice rang out from the trees on the hill above the boatmen, and four older Indian men emerged.

Through the interpreter, Thompson called to the elderly men and spoke to them firmly. "I am surprised these men are behaving in this manner, and I remind you that we promised we would bring supplies, but we will not if we are threatened."

The elderly men spoke, and whatever they said, the confrontation was over. The knives were put away, and under the watchful eyes of the elders the dugouts were soon beyond the first set of cascades, though a number of the Indians stood by and refused to help.

"We may be in for a spot of trouble," Thompson announced to his men. "The worst of the cascades are just ahead." He nodded to Pareil. "Take four armed men and follow with Mr. Stuart as best you can whilst the rest of us hasten to get our canoe beyond those rapids. We'll return to help you."

Quickly fastening a line to their canoe, the men on the riverbank guided it through the water until the rocks were too numerous and they were forced to drag it ashore and uphill beyond the rapids, then down once more to the water. There they found a tremendous flat rock thrusting out into the river. Protected from attack on three sides, they felt much safer. Thompson ordered Peter and Boulard to stay behind and guard the canoe while he and the rest of the men returned to Stuart. Before they could leave, however, across the river, on a steep slope, three rows of warriors appeared. They were armed with bows and arrows.

"Monsieur," Charles hissed, "I am thinking these use arrows that have poison."

Thompson scarcely turned his head. "Take your places about three feet apart and choose your man. Their arrows are notched, but don't fire unless they raise them and pull."

The minutes slid by with agonizing slowness, and Peter's arms ached with holding the heavy musket straight out in front of him. Mosquitoes buzzed in front of his eyes and landed in the sweat on his face, but he forced himself to ignore them as all the men did. Everyone remained absolutely still.

Chapter 18

It must have been a full half-hour before the Indians began to move back up the slope behind them and the muskets could be lowered. There was a bit of shaky laughter as each man hastened to slap the bugs on his face and hands.

Almost immediately, Thompson and his voyageurs disappeared to help the men of Fort Astoria. For Peter the wilderness around them had become too quiet, and he wished now he had been one of those chosen to help. Perhaps the Natives hadn't left and would attack the men as they dragged the dugouts.

As the minutes passed, Boulard, too, became anxious, and to Peter's horror, he said, "It is safe here. I will go only a small way to look over the rocks to find our friends."

Peter nodded, heart in his throat, and then grinned in relief when a dugout appeared, followed by another and another, each dragged by eight men. When all were safe on the rock ledge, Stuart dropped down to sit at its edge and pull off his boots and socks. Dangling his feet in the water, he spoke glumly. "We hid the last boat as best we could, and I say to the devil with it. There's naught in it worth risking a life to save."

As Peter expected, the mapmaker didn't agree. "No matter a man's colour, he should not profit by evil and treachery."

The next morning, when Peter awoke to the sound of an axe splitting wood, he was told that Thompson and Stuart had taken seven of the men down the river to retrieve the boat left behind.

"Me, I believe they are troubled in the head," Boulard said as he stirred the fire. "But David, he would leave nothing behind for those who do wrong."

As the sun brightened the hills, the dugout and the men appeared. After a quick breakfast of boiled salmon, they were on their way. For Peter it wasn't soon enough.

Two very small canoes, each paddled by two young warriors, began to follow less than an hour after the brigade pushed out into the river. They called out words Peter didn't understand and were answered by a chorus of voices coming from the trees ahead at the edge of the water. The river was almost a thousand yards wide now, but the current running against them was strongest in the middle, making it necessary at times to paddle uncomfortably close to the shore.

"No need for concern," Thompson told his men. "I recall we have five miles or more of flooded meadowland along this river. Those in the woods can't attack us from beyond the floods. The arrows wouldn't reach us."

"And those behind," Pareil added with a chuckle, "the current would push them back if they lifted their paddles to favour us with an arrow in the back."

So they were safe for now, Peter thought, but what if the Indians followed them to where the meadows weren't flooded? He had scarcely finished thinking about that possibility when he saw a stand of pines on a slim spit of high land stretching far out into the river. From that bit of dry land and from the canoes following the brigade, voices called back and forth almost without stopping as the brigade drew near. About a hundred yards from that place of easy ambush, Thompson called out an order. With the paddlers pulling hard against the current that was now broadsiding them, the five boats made an abrupt turn and angled for the opposite shore. Cries of rage and disappointment from the shore floated after them, inspiring large amounts of hilarity among Peter's companions.

Two days later, after an almost sleepless night of swatting mosquitoes and tiny flies, Peter could only grin wearily when they reached a village of friendly Shawpatin Indians. It was here that Stuart decided he would wait for the overland brigade he was supposed to meet. "I believe I'll arrange a trade for lighter boats," he said.

"Of course," Thompson agreed. "I'm certain your overland people will have no trouble finding you here."

Peter hid his grin, knowing the mapmaker was aware Stuart wanted the Nor'Westers to get ahead so he could go on to the place where he was to build a trading post. Judging by Stuart's red face, he, too, knew Thompson hadn't been fooled. Nevertheless, the two men shook hands, and there were shouts of *"Au revoir"* until they were out of sight.

Peter's spirits were high as the men paddled easily up the sand-bottomed side of the fast-flowing river. "We're going home," he whispered in Dog's ear. Tentatively, he put his hand on her head and was rewarded with a rumble deep in her throat. With a sigh Peter put his elbows on his knees and his chin in his hands and peered down at the dog. She glanced up at him once, then looked away.

Behind Peter, Boulard said, "Perhaps it is only that she wishes to take part in your conversation and with that sound gives you the answer."

With gratitude in his eyes, Peter turned and gazed at the smiling man. Boulard always knew what to say to make him feel better. He liked the big voyageur better than anyone he knew. And Dog, of course. It was good to have two friends. He leaned sideways in the canoe and let his hand trail in the water as he studied the high walls of the canyons. They took shape, each different from the other as the canoe passed. Some were tall, rounded cones of basalt, gleaming in the sun, and others were jagged rocks with fine, knifelike edges that threatened them as they approached. The sun was warm, and there was plenty to eat. Each of the four villages where they stopped had supplied them with salmon, which though small were very tasty. But he looked forward to arriving at the Snake River where they would change their mode of travel. Thompson wanted to leave the river for a time and go to Spokane House where he hoped to find Finan McDonald.

It took three days to travel up the Snake to its confluence with the smaller Palouse River. Camped beside it was a large Nez Perce village. Thompson immediately smoked with the headmen and gave them news from the other villages that they were always eager to hear. He did this without an interpreter, since he understood and spoke their language, something the Natives seemed to appreciate very much. Thompson spoke of the huge ocean and the condition of the Indians far south. Judging by his voice and gestures, Peter thought the mapmaker must have given an exciting account of the conflict with the hostile Natives they had encountered, for the listening men reacted with horrified expressions.

When Thompson had no more news to report, he told the village elders they had come by canoe more than three hundred miles and must go another four hundred to Kettle Falls. From there he would again travel by canoe to reach the place where he would find the boats loaded with goods for them and the villages below. Then he asked if they had horses they could sell so that he and his men could be on their way.

The headmen informed Thompson that they could spare one horse for each man and one for carrying, but they didn't wish payment. The horses were a present.

After two days of steady riding, they arrived at Spokane House — built close to the Little Spokane River — and were greeted by Finan McDonald. Thompson looked around the long log-built trade room and nodded his approval. Bundles of furs were stacked neatly against the wall, and the rough wooden floor was swept clean. Peter decided they had been expected.

"So it's back you are," McDonald said.

"It would appear," Thompson said dryly. "I see the brigade from east of the mountains isn't here. Have you any word of them at all?"

"William Henry sent word from Athabasca Pass with an Iroquois messenger to ask if any had heard from you," McDonald replied. "But he said nothing about a brigade." He handed Thompson a small stack of mail and invited him and his men to supper.

Thompson accepted the mail without opening it and responded to the invitation by saying, "If you've women here to wash our clothes whilst we have a bath in the river, we would appreciate that, as well."

With Dog by his side Peter found a deep pool guarded by large rocks and leaped into the water. It was cool and soothing, instantly washing away the gritty sand from his hot skin. Most of the ride had been across a treeless plain with a high wind blowing the dust and sand into eyes, nose, and mouth. Now, while Dog paddled back and forth in the quiet pool, Peter allowed himself to hang in it, barely treading water. He closed his eyes and wondered how and where he had learned to swim. Then, suddenly, he realized that for many weeks he hadn't had one of the disturbing visions that had left him too quickly to see them clearly. Nor had he even thought about his memory loss. Perhaps, he reasoned, it was because he had some memories now — ones made on this journey. And he also had friends. Although these were comforting thoughts, Peter knew they weren't enough.

His eyes flew open when a large rock hit the water by his side. Boulard sat on the river's grassy bank. "You are not a fish," he said. "The ragout is prepared, and if you wish to dine, you must put on trousers. If you attend as you are, you will disgrace us."

In reply Peter splashed water on Boulard. Then he whistled for Dog and climbed out of the water. As he reached for his shirt to dry himself, he asked, "How soon will we leave here?"

Boulard turned his hands palm up and shrugged. "I think maybe soon, maybe not. Once more we must first make our way on the horse to Kettle Falls. *Mon ami*, you understand it is important for David to be certain of the place where this Columbia River begins. How else will he know if his maps are true?"

"It's also important that we get through the mountains as soon as we can," Peter insisted.

Boulard cocked his head doubtfully. "There may be difficulties. David has said if no one has been sent to take his place, he must himself make certain the goods in the brigade are sent to the people down the big river."

Peter frowned. "What brigade?"

"Do you not recall from Boat Encampment that David made the message on a piece of bark for our men to take to William Henry who was to send it on to the east? In this message David requests much trade goods to be brought to Kettle Falls for all the Columbia District."

"Trade goods ..." Peter said thoughtfully. "Does that mean we'll have to go down the river again?"

Boulard's reply was a shrug, and he turned away as he heard Vallade calling his name. Left alone, Peter felt a wave of fatigue wash over him. But after giving the matter some thought, he reminded himself that there was nothing waiting for him east of the mountains, and at least here, with the brigade, he was with friends.

They arrived at Kettle Falls in the last days of August after riding through a lush green countryside with forests and narrow brooks of swiftly running, sparkling water. There were almost fifty tents lined up above the falls, mostly Okanagans and members of the Spokane tribe. All were friendly and outdid themselves in singing and dancing for Thompson and his men. These were good people, Peter thought, as bowl after bowl of food was offered to him.

The next day, when the search for wood for the canoe began, the women and children joined in the hunt. As usual it was impossible to find good birch, and they had to settle for cedar found upriver. In two weeks the canoe was built and they were ready to leave.

Thompson, however, ignored the complaints from his crew and insisted they wait. "I've sent Finan McDonald up the river to see if the men from the east have lost their way," he explained.

McDonald arrived a few days later, weary and discouraged. He reported he had travelled two hundred miles without sighting the brigade. Thompson listened, his expression grim. To Boulard he said, "William Henry would have pointed the way through the pass, and in my letter to him I outlined a course to follow to Kettle Falls once that was accomplished." He stood silently, biting his lip, then continued. "If I erred in my judgment that the Columbia River flows west from Boat Encampment, they would miss us here. If that's true, they may be some time finding their way to one of our trading houses."

Boulard pulled on his beard thoughtfully. "Then, *mon ami*, it is my belief to relieve this concern we must ourselves ascend this river to learn if it will lead us to Boat Encampment. If it is not on this river, it will be on another, and we may find someone who has observed our brigade."

It was tireless Pareil who sat behind Peter in the canoe this time, but even he could be heard muttering, "One believes after finding where this miserable river meets the ocean that we have finished our task but, no, we must also advance to the beginning. Instead of returning to our loved ones, we must now search for a brigade that may not even yet be west of the mountains."

Later, when the first flakes of snow fell on their heads, Pareil spoke into Peter's ear. "At the beginning of this great journey we thought to be east of the mountains in August, and already it is September."

Peter nodded but didn't reply. He was sure the men wouldn't want to go down another river looking for the brigade after they reached the top of this one, and he wondered what Thompson would do if they refused.

The river was as difficult to ascend as Boulard had warned it would be. Hunched against sleet or sweating under a burning sun, the men laboured twelve hours a day, every day. Even when the wind was behind and they could put up sail, the paddlers strained to keep the canoe moving against the strong current. Each night they camped at about six o'clock, and while Thompson took his usual sightings of the horizon, a few of the men went hunting. And the hunting was good. There were flocks of geese picking in the grass in the meadows, and ducks swam back and forth on every backwater of the river. Peter set his traps, and more often than not there was rabbit for breakfast. Even though they carried no flour or fat, hunger wasn't a problem.

On the twelfth day of travel Peter found himself

nauseated, and his head ached, but he said nothing. By the time they camped for the night, Peter's condition became obvious to all when he stumbled ashore and threw up everything he had eaten that day. "Best have some tea," Thompson suggested, then picked up his box of instruments and walked up a barren hill close to the river.

"Don't want anything," Peter mumbled, reaching into the canoe for his bedroll. There was no grass near their campsite, only sand and small stones, but though he felt better now, he was too tired to care. Spreading his blankets on the ground, he stretched out and closed his eyes.

Peter dozed, waking once when Dog whined and poked him in the ear with her nose. He waved her away and went to sleep again until dusk and light from the flames of the campfire danced across his face. He felt much better, hungry even. He stirred, and as he leaned on one elbow preparing to sit up, he stiffened with fear. Not two feet from his face a long, very black snake was coiled.

"Don't move, Peter," Boulard's voice called out softly. "Don't move, and you will be —"

Peter felt a rush of air and hair brush his face as Dog hurtled by. He leaped to his feet, peered into the dusk, and saw Thompson and Côté hammer the hapless snake with the butts of their muskets. Dog stood near the men, her head hanging down. Peter tried to run to her, but Boulard held him back. "Wait, Peter, she received a bite, I think, and it is possible the tooth remains that will poison you if you touch it."

Pushing Boulard aside, Peter knelt by his dog. She

fell to her knees and then onto her side. It was Thompson who crouched beside him, and as Dog lay with her eyes closed, he carefully examined her legs and stomach. Lifting her front foot, he pointed to a tiny drop of blood. Peter stared at it in horror. "Can't you do something? Can't you take out the poison?"

Thompson got to his feet and took his kerchief from his neck. "Even if she were my own child, Peter, I could do little except to tie off the foot above the bite and try to squeeze out the poison. That we'll do, and we must make certain she remains quiet. Perhaps the snake has struck something else recently and had little poison for your friend. We must wait."

Taking his knife from his belt, Thompson nodded to Boulard, who secured Dog's head firmly under his arm and ordered Peter to hold her legs. Dog struggled weakly when the mapmaker's knife sliced a small cross over the snakebite, but she didn't cry out.

"Come, Peter," Boulard said when the task was finished. "We will shake out your bedroll.

Peter followed numbly. It was his fault that Dog was dying. He had been warned not to put his bedroll down until after dark, for by then the snakes would have found a place to sleep for the night and wouldn't emerge until morning after the dew had dried. When he returned to Dog's side, he saw Charles on his knees patting a handful of black mud on her leg. "What ...?" Peter began when Charles looked up.

"Mud good for bite," the Iroquois said.

Peter nodded and tried to smile. He was grateful that Charles was trying to help, but somehow he was certain mud wouldn't do any good.

The voices around the campfire were low that night while Peter sat up on his bedroll with Dog beside him. One by one the men retired to their own beds, and when Peter's head began to nod, Boulard put another piece of wood on the dimming fire. "Sleep now, *mon ami*. Tomorrow will arrive soon."

Peter slid down beside Dog to stare at the sky. There had to be animals up there, he reasoned, then wondered if Dog would recognize him when they next met. He dozed and awoke each time Dog quivered beside him. Near dawn she cried out and her feet thrashed frantically. Peter sat up quickly and gathered her into his arms. She stiffened, then relaxed with a whine deep in her throat. Sobbing into her fur, Peter gently stroked her back and her sides. She stirred then and lifted her head to lick his face once before her head dropped.

Unable to bear the pain he felt, Peter squeezed his eyes shut and rocked back and forth, holding his friend. It was then that the misty vision appeared again. This time he saw himself on a boat slowly sailing from a green shore. People were waving, and nearby a dog sat watching him. It was smaller than Dog and didn't have long hair, though it was black and white. He tried to cry out, and the vision disappeared.

Peter was hardly aware that someone had crept to his side and wrapped his arms around him. When he opened his eyes, he saw that it was Thompson.

"She died," Peter croaked, "and it's my fault."

Thompson released him and lifted Dog's head. He frowned, then put his hand on her side. "Not yet, Peter. I feel her heartbeat. She is but asleep."

During the night, both Côté and Pareil were

overcome with the same sickness Peter had experienced, and though they were better in the morning, they were too weak to go on. Thompson announced he would leave supplies with the two men, and the rest would continue the journey. His face wore a glum expression as he sat cross-legged by the fire. "We're now on the same longitude as the North Saskatchewan. If we don't come to Boat Encampment within two days more, I'll have failed."

"Failed?" Vallade echoed.

"Of course," Boulard said. "You recall David has said he would know where the Columbia River begins when we once again see Boat Encampment."

Vallade nodded doubtfully.

Remembering how kind Thompson had been the night before, Peter prayed that he would be allowed to stay behind and care for Dog as well as the two men. As if reading his mind, Thompson glanced at Peter. "We're short two men now. You're needed to help with the paddling."

Chapter 19

There was no singing, and the men talked little for the next day and a half, but when they reached the big bend of the Columbia, a cheer went up from every throat. The rough shelter they had built was sighted. Boat Encampment! As they turned to shore, Thompson leaped from the canoe into the knee-deep water and threw up his arms. "It's done," he cried. "For twenty-seven years I've strived to map this most wondrous of countries from sea to sea and from north to south. My efforts are over."

They made camp early, and after a search for some sort of message from the missing brigade, Thompson took out his journal and began to write feverishly. Some of the men went hunting, and for the first time in weeks they dined on moose and big, ripe blackberries found in a nearby patch.

Although he had accepted that Dog wouldn't be alive when he returned, Peter couldn't rid himself of a glimmer of hope, and he half dreaded the return to their campsite. Thompson, however, had other plans. He was determined to find the brigade. "We'll leave a message on a tree and one in the shed," he said, "and paddle a distance up Canoe River. They might not have understood the rough map I sent and by mistake followed the Canoe after they came through the pass."

As they poled and paddled against the current, Peter felt the beginnings of despair. He had thought he would be happy when this journey came to an end, but now it didn't matter. Peter had lost Dog, and soon he would lose another friend, for Boulard had spoken often of finding a female to his liking who would cook and sew for him for the rest of his days while he hunted and fished. And what was in store for him? he wondered. Peter tried to find encouragement in Boulard's promise to ask if the company might use him as a clerk at a post somewhere. He sighed, hoping he would be among strangers who wouldn't have to be told he had no name.

After three days and almost fifty miles up the Canoe, they camped in the early afternoon to decide whether or not to go on. Thompson admitted he wasn't sure what they should do. As every man, except Peter, offered an opinion, a canoe appeared with two men in it. *"Monsieur!"* they called out even before they reached the shore. "Mr. Henry, he waits with the goods. We arrived by horse to find your letter soon after you left."

Thompson broke into laughter. "By thunder, it didn't occur to me you'd come by horse."

It took just a few minutes to break camp and hop into the canoe. The three-day trip they had made up the Canoe River took only a few hours to fly with the current downstream to Boat Encampment.

"You old scoundrel!" the usually quiet William Henry shouted at Thompson as Charles manoeuvred the canoe to shore. "You truly are amazing. I thought I'd find you buried somewhere, but here you are." As Thompson got out of the canoe, William clapped him on the back. "Have you been to the ocean yet, or have you been paddling around here enjoying the sun?"

Thompson raised his eyebrows. "If you can read, sir, you can see from my note that we've reached the Pacific and are on our way back." He pointed to the bend of the Columbia. "The headwaters of this river are down near where we built Kootenay House."

William appeared startled, then he laughed. "Are you saying had we known we could have used this route years before?"

Thompson nodded. "And avoided much of the trouble with the Peigans."

Listening, Peter felt a small wave of happiness. No matter what happened to him, he would always remember that he had been with the explorer who had found an important route to the sea.

The two men moved in the direction of the campfire, Thompson talking enthusiastically until he stopped in mid-sentence. Then, raising his voice, he asked, "And where did you two come from? And how did you get here?"

Peter turned to see Côté and Pareil emerge grinning from one of the tents. "We wished to surprise you," Côté said. "In one day we no longer suffered *malade*, and Pareil, here, traded his cap for us to be passengers of a fellow who came by in his canoe." When the rest of the men finished greeting the two, Côté continued. "He wanted my cap, too, in exchange for taking the dog also, but I offered to help him paddle."

Peter wasn't certain he had heard right. *Dog? What dog?* Côté and Pareil looked at him and grinned widely. Beckoning for Peter to follow, Pareil led him to a stout cottonwood behind his tent where Dog was tied. She leaped to her feet and barked a welcome, her tail wagging crazily. Peter was too stunned to move. She was very thin, but her eyes were bright and her nose appeared to be damp. In a moment Peter was on his knees beside her, petting her roughly, happily realizing she didn't seem to mind. In fact, she seemed to like it!

When later he returned to the campfire, Peter saw that the horses had been unloaded and the packs of trade goods stacked in the mapmaker's canoe. Would they now have to go back down the river to distribute them? Peter wondered. But Thompson had drawn a rough map for William Henry to follow to Spokane House and directions for Finan McDonald to take the goods downstream. To his own men he said, "I'll ride east over the mountains to get the goods Mr. Henry couldn't bring. Who will volunteer to stay here and build a stout canoe and, for double the pay, go back downriver with me to Spokane House when I return?"

To Peter's astonishment, as one man, the entire crew stepped forward. After a moment's hesitation, he did so himself. The corners of Thompson's mouth turned up briefly, and he shook his head. "No, Boulard. I prefer that you go beyond the Athabasca post and take care of a matter for me." He said nothing to Peter.

Two days later Peter was glad to see Young Joseph, their Iroquois guide, appear as they were getting ready to leave. There would be six of them now to lead the horses back through the pass and load them again so once more they could slog through the snow on the return to the Columbia River.

Chapter 20

The journey through the mountains wasn't as bad as Peter had expected, though the snow was often up to the bellies of the horses and his snowshoes cut into his feet. Still, there were no rain or snowstorms, and when their rations ran short, they ate less. These hardships were quickly forgotten when they reached William Henry's snug cabin. Although he wasn't there, his two men were overjoyed to see Thompson and his companions, for they were bored and hungry for talk. Not interested in hearing tales about their journey, Peter went outside in the fresh air to admire the surroundings.

The light snow of the night before had turned into a thin drizzle of rain, but the clouds were separating now and moving eastward. The air was heady with the scent of damp pine trees, their green tips thrusting high above the smaller gold and orange aspen and birch. With Dog following, Peter walked down to where a lusty stream poured into the shallow Athabasca River and saw a rainbow arc from one mountain to another, painting the snowcaps in iridescent colours. It was so beautiful that he felt he had to share it with Boulard. As he tried to turn and run at the same time, his foot slipped on a rock on the edge of the stream, and he fell. When his head struck, he felt it explode.

It was dark when Peter awoke. Dog was lying on her side, her back pressed against him. Absently, he patted her head, and she sighed contentedly. With his other hand he felt around him. He was on the floor of a cabin wearing a shirt that seemed to come to his knees and was covered by blankets. There was a great ache in his head. Slowly, he began to remember his fall on the rocks. Slowly, he felt his frozen memory start to thaw. Slowly, he began to recall many things.

His lips formed the words, but he made no sound. *My name is Adam — Adam Barrett.* He rubbed his forehead. *I thought when I remembered I would be happy. Why do I have this feeling of dread?* The dread mounted as images of a rolling ship forced their way into his mind, and he felt the lashing rain as men cried out in the darkness.

Beside him, Dog leaped to her feet as Peter squeezed his eyes shut and rocked from side to side, trying to blot out the vision. But he couldn't. It came with the explosion of thunder and a flash of white lightning that hung in the night sky, illuminating the ship and his father crawling toward him on the slippery deck. He felt himself clinging to the rail and stretching his hand into the darkness that followed, but no one was there. And when next the lightning danced across the boiling sea the deck was empty.

Peter turned his face toward the rough log cabin wall. Giving himself up to the pain in his heart, he allowed the tears to come. All the while he cried, Dog whined softly and poked her nose in the back of his neck. When he couldn't weep anymore, he wiped his eyes and nose on his sleeve and allowed the memories to begin again.

I lived in a village in England, and I had a dog — not much like Dog, but it was white, too, and had black spots. He squeezed his eyes shut, trying to recall his mother, but he couldn't. Peter knew he had been very small when she died. But before that she had given him the puppy. He remembered the puppy growing quickly into a playful friend. Together they often crept into the forbidden woods, for the land belonged to the lord in the manor house. He set snares for rabbits and grouse to supplement the meagre fare on their dinner table.

Peter smiled a little, remembering. *I was almost caught once, and would have been, if the path hadn't been covered with ice. The groundskeeper slipped and fell, but my bare feet kept me up straight.* He rubbed his burning eyes in the darkness. His father had been tall and lean and had taught school. It was a small school in a tiny village surrounded by farmland where men worked hard to make the small profits they had to share with the lord. Peter's throat tightened as he realized that was the reason they had been on the ship. They were sailing to America where his father was to teach in another country school not far from a city called Boston.

Peter opened his eyes. It was half-light now, and someone was moving near the long table. A candle sputtered, and in its glow he spied David Thompson. The mapmaker moved closer and knelt beside Peter. "Are you having a dream, lad?"

Peter shook his head and turned away. His heart ached for his father. A hand touched his shoulder, and he turned back to see understanding in the mapmaker's eyes.

"You remember then," he said. When Peter nodded, he sat cross-legged on the floor and placed the candle beside him. "I hoped it wouldn't happen in this fashion, Peter. I had planned another way."

The words cut through Peter's sorrow, and he sat up, leaning on his elbow the better to see Thompson. "What do you mean, 'another way'?"

For a moment the mapmaker didn't reply. Then, as though choosing his words carefully, he said, "At Spokane House I received letters from the east. I found one from Montreal that informed me they had news of a schooner bound for Boston that went down in a storm more than two years past. Three of the crew, still alive, were picked up by an American ship."

Peter wet his lips and spoke past the knot in his throat. "It was the *Windrover.*"

"Aye, and one of the men said they had carried two passengers — a man and his son."

"I tried to find my father, but the first mate pulled me away. He said he was gone, and I heard the mast cracking. I woke up in a boat." Peter blinked, his heart hurting as well as his head. "Why didn't you tell me?"

"Perhaps I erred, Peter, but I thought it best to wait until our journey's end and try then to bring back your memory slowly. I thought first to mention the name Barrett to see if that would help you win it back, and if not, I would add the little I knew. Perhaps I was wrong. I hoped to save you from a great shock."

Wearily, Peter said, "Thank you, sir. I think I'd like to sleep now."

When he awoke, it was late afternoon and the cabin was empty. Even Dog had disappeared, and so had much of the pain in his head. Despite the sadness in his heart, he was hungry. He lay still, thinking. Peter would mourn his father for a very long while, but right now he must think of the days ahead. It was time to ask Thompson about the possibility of gaining employment with the North West Company at a post somewhere. He knew it couldn't be Montreal, for only very senior company men worked there. Peter would miss the men he had spent the past year with, especially Boulard, but he had no other choice. He was a man now and must look after himself.

Ignoring a stab of pain, Peter steadied himself against the wall and rose to his feet. At the same moment the door opened, and Thompson walked in, followed by Boulard. With hurried steps they reached his side and grabbed an arm to lead him to the table. "Best be careful, lad," the mapmaker said. "I feel certain that head of yours won't welcome another fall."

Boulard looked down at Peter sympathetically. "Ah, my young friend, I fear now to see you leave my sight else you do more damage to your head."

Peter tried to grin, then swallowed hard, telling himself it was time to be bold and speak as a man. "Sir, now that we're at the end of our journey I have a great favour to ask you." He swallowed again. "I must find work. If you have need of a man in one of your posts, would you consider me?"

The two men glanced at each, their eyes twinkling. It was Thompson who replied. "Boulard and I have been discussing that very thing. However, we don't think a post on the prairie is suitable for someone who's been a voyageur."

"You don't?" Peter was puzzled by the mapmaker's light tone.

Thompson chuckled. "To be serious, Peter, I should tell you that while we were at Boat Encampment both Boulard and I were impressed with the ease with which you managed to teach letters and a beginning of reading to some of our voyageurs. We're certain you have the makings of a fine schoolmaster, and if you wish, we'll see that you become one."

Peter's heart leaped. A schoolmaster! "It ... it's what my father wished for me. It's why we left England. He thought in the New World ..." He was overwhelmed and couldn't continue.

Thompson glanced at Boulard, who grinned. "I take it he agrees. Here's our plan. You and Boulard will go on to Montreal with the next brigade heading east. I'll give you a letter for Mr. Fraser. He'll help you to find a school to finish your education, and you and Boulard will live on the farm I purchased three years earlier. My family and I will join you next year."

Peter turned his back until he thought it safe to speak. The silence was broken by Boulard. "It has a good sound, this name Adam Barrett, but for me I believe always he will be Peter."

Scrubbing the moisture from his eyes, Peter looked up. "Then I'll no longer be Peter No-Name. I'll be Peter Three-Names — Peter Adam Barrett."

David Thompson smiled his agreement. "Aye, and later to have a fourth — Peter Adam Barrett, Schoolmaster."

David Thompson Chronology

1770	David Thompson is born in London, England, to Welsh parents.
1784	Thompson apprentices to Hudson's Bay Company at fourteen years old and boards a ship for Canada.
1788	He breaks his leg and, while recovering, learns surveying and astronomy.
1790–96	Thompson surveys much of northern Manitoba and Saskatchewan.
1797	He joins the North West Company, the Hudson's Bay Company's rival.
1798	Thompson surveys 4,200 miles from Grand Portage through Lake Winnipeg to the headwaters of the Assiniboine River and Missouri River and two sides of Lake Superior.
1799	He marries Charlotte Small at Île-à-la-Crosse.
1800–01	Thompson makes his first attempt to find a route across the Rocky Mountains.
1802–06	He surveys on the Peace River and Lake Athabasca.
1807	Thompson crosses the Rockies via Howse Pass.
1808–09	He explores the Kootenay and Spokane Rivers and establishes trading posts in what are now British Columbia, Washington, Oregon, Idaho, and Montana.

1810	On his way back from the West, Thompson receives orders to turn around and make another trip through the Rockies with the express purpose of following the Columbia River from its source to where it flows into the Pacific Ocean.
1811	Thompson crosses the Rockies by Athabasca Pass and travels down the Kootenay River to join the Columbia River and then continues to the Columbia's estuary.
1812	He retires from the fur trade and, with his family, moves to Terrebonne, north of Montreal.
1814	Thompson completes his most famous map of northwestern North America.
1817	He surveys the Canada/U.S. border from Lake of the Woods to the Eastern Townships in what is now Quebec.
1843	Thompson completes work on his atlas of the area from Hudson Bay to the Pacific.
1843–50	He begins writing his adventures using his seventy-seven original notebooks, but never completes the work.
1857	Thompson dies in Montreal at the age of eighty-six. Charlotte dies three months later.

SELECTED READING

Bond, Rowland. *The Original Northwester: David Thompson and the Native Tribes of North America.* Nine Mile Falls, WA: Spokane House Enterprises, 1972.

Campbell, Marjorie Wilkins. T*he Nor'westers: The Fight for the Fur Trade.* Calgary: Fifth House Publishers, 2002.

Garrod, Stan. *David Thompson.* Toronto: Grolier, 1989.

Jenish, D'Arcy. *Epic Wanderer: David Thompson and the Mapping of the Canadian West.* Toronto: Anchor Canada, 2004.

McCart, J. (Joyce). *On the Road with David Thompson.* Calgary: Fifth House Publishers, 2000.

Nisbet, Jack. *The Mapmaker's Eye: David Thompson on the Columbia Plateau.* Pullman, WA: Washington State University Press, 2005.

Pole, Graeme. *David Thompson: The Epic Expeditions of a Great Canadian Explorer.* Canmore, AB: Altitude Publishing, 2003.

Savage, Marie. *Early Voyageurs: The Incredible Adventures of the Fearless Fur Traders.* Canmore, AB: Altitude Publishing, 2003.

Shardlow, Tom. *David Thompson: A Trail by Stars. Montreal*: XYZ Publishing, 2006.

Thompson, David. *Columbia Journals, Bicentennial Edition.* Ed. Barbara Belyea. Montreal and Kingston: McGill-Queen's University Press, 2007.

Twigg, Alan. *Thompson's Highway: British Columbia's Fur Trade.* Vancouver, BC: Ronsdale Press, 2006.

Van Herk, Aritha. "Travels with Charlotte." *Canadian Geographic* 127:4 (July/August 2007).